W9-BAK-306

Cecilia's year

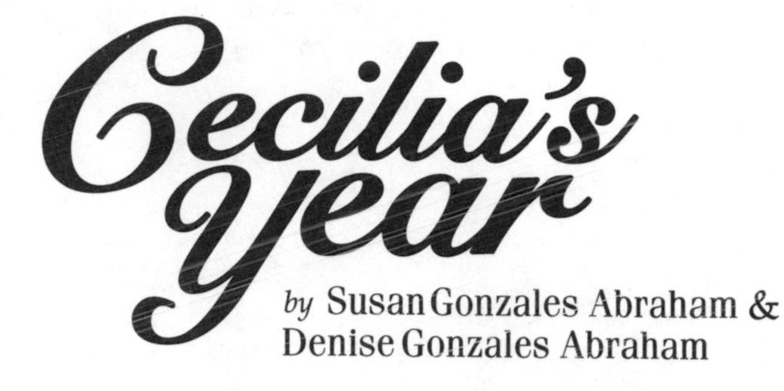

Cecilia's year

by Susan Gonzales Abraham &
Denise Gonzales Abraham

CINCO PUNTOS PRESS
El Paso, Texas

 For further information, write Cinco Puntos Press, 701 Texas Avenue, El Paso, TX 79901; or call 1-915-838-1625.

FIRST EDITION
10 9 8 7 6 5 4 3 2 1

Library of Congress Cataloging-in-Publication Data

Abraham, Susan Gonzales, 1951-
Cecilia's year / by Susan and Denise Gonzales Abraham.— 1st ed.
p. cm.
Summary: Nearly fourteen and poor, Cecilia Gonzales wants desperately to go to high school and become a teacher until her mother's old-fashioned ideas about a woman's place threaten her dreams.
ISBN 0-938317-87-3 (alk. paper)
[1. Family life—New Mexico—Fiction. 2. Schools—Fiction. 3. Farm life—New Mexico—Fiction. 4. Sex role—Fiction. 5. Books and reading—Fiction. 6. New Mexico—History—20th century—Fiction.] I. Abraham, Denise Gonzales, 1949- II. Title.
PZ7.A1665Ce 2004
[Fic]—dc22

2004013374

Thanks to Jessica Powers for introducing
Cinco Puntos to YA books.
Special thanks to
Celia Gonzales Bencomo and Adolfo Gonzales.

Cover art by Gaspar Enriquez
Cover and book design by Paco Casas

Hats off to sisters everywhere!

Dedicated to the children of
José and Josefina Gonzales

Elías, Cecilia, Robert, Adolfo,
Celia & Belia

Junio

"Cecilia! Ceciliaaaaa! *¿Dónde estás?* Where are you? You are supposed to be helping me with supper! *¡Ándale!*"

Cecilia heard Mamá's angry voice and looked up from the book she was reading to see Mamá's thin, tight face at the kitchen window. "*¡Ya vengo, Mamá!*" Cecilia shouted. "I'm coming."

She quickly closed the book she was reading, using a long blade of grass to save her place. She stood up, brushing grass and dirt from her thin cotton dress. "I'm coming!" she called out again. She knew it wasn't wise to keep Mamá waiting.

For the last hour María Cecilia Gonzales had been lost in

a long-ago time, helping Betty Zane save the fort from an Indian attack. It seemed to her that daily chores and demands were always interrupting the best part of the book she was reading. Now she would have to wait until supper was eaten, the dishes were washed, and the children put to bed before she could lose herself once again in the exciting Zane Grey story.

Cecilia looked longingly at the soft patch of clover where she had been sitting. It was her favorite spot, under the ancient cottonwood tree on the other side of the narrow irrigation canal that separated the house from the fields. The soft, spongy clover made a perfect seat for reading or day-dreaming or just looking up at the clouds.

Running as fast as she could in her bare feet, Cecilia reached the kitchen door and quickly pulled her apron off its hook and tied it around her waist. Mamá always insisted she wear an apron to protect her dresses. New dresses were hard to come by when there were so many mouths to feed, the doctor's bills to pay, and a farm mortgage to meet. Cecilia hadn't had a new everyday dress since school had started in September, and it was now June.

"Where have you been, *hija*? You know what time we start preparing supper. Your papá and the boys will be in for their *cena* soon, and you're off somewhere reading those worthless books of yours."

"Mamá, my books are my treasures! They're wonderful! I learn so many new things from them. How can you call them worthless?" Cecilia protested.

"Because they *are* worthless," her mother answered. "What does a farm girl need with books? You are filling your head with nonsense. Everything you need to know you can learn from your family. Your books can't help us put supper on the table. Only our hard work and our prayers can do that."

"But, Mamá, you know I need to read and learn everything I can before I go to high school next year," Cecilia said.

"*If* you go to high school. Your papá and I are not so sure that is what is best for you. You need to concentrate on learning how to run a home—how to cook and sew and feed the children you will have, my grandchildren. Your books will only bring you unhappiness by making you want things you cannot have."

"Mamá, I just want to go to high school. I want it more than anything else in the world. *Es mi sueño*. It's my only dream!" Cecilia cried.

"You see, there you go again with that nonsense! You don't need dreams. Dreams are not going to help you be a good wife and mother. You need to learn how to work hard and make do. Your books are a luxury we can't afford. Believe me, your future husband isn't going to care if you went to high school. What he will care about is coming home after a hard day in the fields to a good mother for his children and a hot supper on the table," Mamá warned. "Now set the table. You know your chores come first," Mamá ordered as she set a pot of *frijoles* on the wood stove.

"I'm sorry, Mamá. It won't happen again. I promise. *Perdóname.*" Cecilia knew this was not the time to argue. Mamá was tired and in a bad mood, and there was work to be done. She would bring up the subject of high school at a better time.

Cecilia and her mother had had this same argument many times before, and there seemed to be no resolution. Mamá simply did not understand Cecilia's strong desire to go to high school, to be something different from all the other farm girls. Somehow Cecilia had to make Mamá realize how important high school was to her and convince her to change her mind. But she knew this would not be easy. When Mamá made up her mind about something, she rarely changed it. And Mamá was adamant that Cecilia grow up to be as good a farm woman as she herself was.

Cecilia sighed deeply. "*Ay, Dios*," she whispered to herself, "please help me change Mamá's mind."

Cecilia tried to make amends for her tardiness by setting the table with the blue and white dishes that had been in the family since Mamá and Papá were married. She felt ashamed because she had been reading while Mamá was in the hot kitchen alone doing work that she, Cecilia, should have been doing. As the oldest daughter and almost fourteen, she knew she should be behaving more maturely and helping out around the house more. Mamá and Tía Sara had their hands full taking care of the baby, the washing, the ironing, the cooking, and the hundreds of other chores that are necessary in a farmhouse filled with three adults and six children. Papá and the boys worked hard outside all day, and Cecilia knew her part was to help in the house, even though she would much rather be reading a good book or daydreaming about Johnny Tafoya.

Just thinking about Johnny made butterflies flutter in her stomach. She hadn't seen him since the last day of school in May, but she was sure he would come to visit soon. After all, wasn't he the best friend of her older brother Elías? Elías didn't know how she felt about Johnny. If he did, he would tease her unmercifully. And worse, he might tell Johnny! So Cecilia had to behave as calmly and coolly as she could whenever Johnny was around.

The table was set. Cecilia felt a warm glow as she looked around the large kitchen that served as the central gathering place for her family. Cecilia loved this old adobe house that had been built by her grandfather many years before. Her mother had been born in this house, and Cecilia too had been born in the bedroom with the pink-flowered wallpaper. Cecilia was most proud of the parlor, with its corner fireplace and the beautiful mahogany piano that Mamá's father had ordered all the way from St. Louis, Missouri. But most of all, Cecilia loved the kitchen. It was the heart of the house and the family. The adobe walls were plastered and whitewashed. The wooden floor was worn from the thousands of footsteps made by the family over the years. Mamá had glued decals of red cherry clusters on the white kitchen cabinets and on the white corner china cabinet. Red-and-white checked curtains covered the two windows which faced the rising sun. Every morning, warm golden rays of sun stretched across the table and floor. And since the wood stove was always burning, the kitchen was the warmest room in the house.

Around the long rectangular table, the family would meet to eat and talk about the day's events. Most of the talk centered around the farm and the work that had to be done—which field had to be plowed, who would be hired on to help with the harvesting of the chile and the cotton crops, or how many chicks should be ordered from the farm catalog. In fact, right now there was a cardboard box next to the stove holding a dozen baby chicks that Papá had brought back in a crate from the train station in Rincón yesterday. Cecilia picked up one of the tiny yellow balls of fluff and held it against her cheek—it was so soft and sweet.

"I wish you would stay this little and soft forever. Mamá, why do the chicks have to get old and big?"

"Ay, *hija*, every living thing has to grow old. It is a part of life. It is God's plan for all of us. Look how big you have grown. Last year you were a little girl, and now look at you! You are taller than I am. You will make a strong wife for a farmer someday."

Cecilia turned to place the chick in the box and also to hide the frown on her face from her mother. She didn't want to be a strong wife for a farmer. She wanted to get a job in an office in a big city. As much as she loved the farm, she dreamed of someday living somewhere big and exciting. She knew the only way to get there was to get an education. That's why it was so important for her to go to high school. In high school she could learn to type and take shorthand. Then she could get a job in a bank or in an office in a tall building—a skyscraper! Maybe she could even be a teacher! The thought of being a teacher in charge of her own classroom filled her with excitement. She would share her love of reading and learning with her students. But would it ever really happen? Could her dreams carry her there? If only Mamá could understand!

Ay, Dios, no sense daydreaming when there was so much work still to be done. Cecilia expertly sliced a loaf of homemade bread into a dozen thick slices. The crusty slices would be used to sop up the last bit of gravy from Mamá's delicious *caldillo.* Tonight Mamá was making everybody's favorite—a stew made with beef and chile, carrots, onions, and potatoes grown in their own garden. There would be *frijoles*, of course, as beans were served at every meal—even breakfast—and a tall pitcher of fresh milk from one of the farm's cows. Fito and Roberto, Cecilia's younger brothers, were in charge of milking the cows every morning and evening.

At least I don't have to milk the cows, Cecilia thought as she got ready for Fito to pour the milk into the pitcher from his bucket.

"Fito, here's the pitcher. Be careful not to spill the milk like you did this morning," Cecilia told Fito as he entered the kitchen with a pail filled with frothy white liquid. But she told him gently because Fito was her favorite among her brothers and sisters.

"*Sí, sí.* I know how to do it. Haven't I been doing it for months now? It was Roberto who made me laugh. That's why I spilled it," Fito explained, trying to save face. Fito was a stocky boy with a ruddy complexion. When he smiled, his hazel eyes squinted into little slits below shaggy brown bangs. He had been a sickly child, but tender care and healthy country air and food had made him outgrow his weakness. Fito had a twin sister, Belia. Belia had been the strong one at birth and always bragged that she was twelve minutes older than Fito. Fito's real name was Adolfo, but that was too long and formal for a farm boy.

"Fito, go tell Tía Sara that supper is ready. And don't forget to wash your hands," Mamá said.

"I'm here already," said Tía Sara as she entered the kitchen. She was carrying baby Sylvia, who was a year and a half old. Sylvia was walking now, but Tía Sara had been bathing her and didn't want her to get dirty. Sylvia had already eaten her supper, so Tía Sara placed her in the wooden high chair that Papá had made and gave her a string of beads to play with. Sylvia was the youngest of the children. Cecilia adored her and had named her after a doll she once had.

"Well then, Fito, go tell your Papá and Roberto that supper is ready. And tell them to wash their hands too," Mamá said. "Where is Belia? *¿Dónde está esa muchachita?*" Mamá asked.

"She's emptying the baby's bath water," said Tía Sara. "The sweet girl was helping me give Sylvia her bath."

"Well, that sweet girl was supposed to be setting the table. That girl will do anything to get out of work in the kitchen," Mamá said with exasperation.

"Oh, Mamá, don't be angry. *No te enojes.* Sylvia is so much fun to bathe. She splashes the water and laughs so much it makes me laugh, too," Cecilia said in defense of her little sister. She knew Belia preferred running wild through the fields with her brothers rather than doing housework. As twins, Belia and Fito were inseparable. It galled Belia that Fito got to be outside with Papá and the boys while she had to sit primly and learn to sew.

At that moment Belia burst into the kitchen from the back door. The front of her dress was completely soaked.

"*Mi hija*, what happened to your dress?" Mamá asked. "Did one of the boys throw water on you?"

"No, Mamá, I was rushing to throw out the baby's bath water, and I tripped and spilled the whole tub on myself!" said Belia. She was near tears because she had also skinned one knee badly.

"*El que anda con apuro, con frequencia se atraza,*" said Tía Sara, who had an appropriate saying, or *dicho*, for every occasion. "You were in a hurry, and now you will be late for supper. Come with me, and we'll change your dress and clean your knee."

Belia went off with Tía Sara, whom all the children loved as a second mother. She was Mamá's younger sister. She had never married, but lived instead with her sister, helping her raise her large brood of children. For Mamá, she was a godsend, as the work in and out of the farmhouse was never-ending. Without Tía Sara to help cook, clean, do laundry, put up fruits and vegetables, and help with the children, Mamá would not have been able to cope.

Cecilia thought Tía Sara was beautiful. She had large dark eyes set deep in her olive face. Her skin was flawless and her nose long and straight. She wore her dark hair tightly braided and wrapped around the back of her head. She was taller than Mamá and had a better sense of humor. She was warm and loving toward the children, whereas Mamá was the disciplinarian. Tía Sara was the one Cecilia ran to when she had a problem.

Tía Sara was the only one who knew of Cecilia's ambition to earn a high school diploma so she could get a job in a big city someday. She seemed to genuinely understand Cecilia's frustration at living in a small farming community so far from museums, libraries, and tall buildings where women worked side by side with men and wore crisp white blouses, dark suits, and high heels. Cecilia would confide in Tía Sara as they sat in their chairs on the porch at night, complaining that Mamá and Papá didn't understand her. Tía Sara would take Cecilia's face in her hands and whisper, "*Ten paciencia, ten paciencia*. Be patient. Things will turn out the way they are supposed to. No matter what we want or plan, God knows best. *El hombre propone y Dios dispone.* If God wants this for you, it will happen."

Cecilia believed her, but the words could not quell the impatience and frustration she felt deep inside. She had read many books about all the wonderful places in the world and all the exciting things to see and hear and taste. Her chest felt like bursting as she thought about being forced to stay on the farm and live the life Mamá and Tía Sara had lived. She loved her home in this quiet Río Grande valley in Derry, New Mexico, surrounded by purple and blue mountains, but sometimes it felt as if the river and the mountains were trapping her here, locking her in, and she would never get out. In her mind she could hear one of Tía Sara's *dichos: Aunque la jaula sea de oro, no deja de ser prisión.* A cage is a cage even if it is made of gold.

"*¡Ay, qué hambre tengo!* I am so hungry I could eat an entire cow by myself!" said Papá as he and the boys came into the kitchen.

"Papá!" cried Cecilia, and she ran to throw herself in his arms and give him a big hug. She hadn't seen him since breakfast. He and the boys had been out in the fields all day. They had even taken their lunches—burritos and apples—with them so they wouldn't have to come back to the house at noon.

"*Mi preciosa*, how are you? What did you do today?" Papá asked Cecilia. Everyone knew he doted on her as his oldest daughter. And Cecilia adored her tall robust father with his red face, dark mustache, and the blue bandanna tied around his neck. Mamá was the strict one, the one who meted out punishments. She was the one who looked at them with piercing dark eyes whenever they misbehaved. But Papá was the fun one, the loving one, the one who picked them up and swung them around or carried them on his shoulders. He loved his babies and cringed from ever having to punish them.

"*Por Dios, Josefina,*" he would tell Mamá. "They are just children. Let them have fun. There is time enough for them to behave when they are adults."

"They may be children, but they are our children, and they must learn to behave and not embarrass us in front of other people," Mamá would answer. And she would be the one to get the *chicote*, the leather strap, and whip the boys on their behinds or the girls on their legs whenever they really did something wrong. Then the children would run to Papá crying, and he would hug them to his chest saying, "*¿Quién le meneuron, quién le menearon?* Who punished you?"

"*Ándale*, come on. Sit down and eat. I have been cooking all afternoon," said Mamá crossly.

Each member of the family took his or her seat around the long wooden table and waited silently for Papá to say grace. As they bowed their heads, Papá said the words he said every evening before supper.

"*Gracias, Señor, por lo que vamos a comer.* Thank you, Lord, for what we are about to eat. May your grace be with us always."

Then everyone seemed to speak at once as Mamá served them her spicy *caldillo* and Tía Sara passed the bread and homemade butter. Belia was regaling Fito with the story of her misadventure with the bath water. Roberto was once more begging Papá for a pocketknife, and baby Sylvia was rattling the wooden beads on her toy. Elías sat quietly eating his *caldillo* with relish. Every day he seemed more and more a man, and less and less a boy. Cecilia ate the spicy, delicious stew and thought no one could cook like her mamá. With pride, she looked around the table, and her eyes rested on each family member—Papá taking a big gulp of coffee from his mug; Mamá sitting straight up in her chair, proper as always; Tía Sara, gentle and beautiful; Elías, her handsome, quiet older brother; Fito and Belia, the talkative, mischievous twins; Roberto, tall for his age, but so thin; and Sylvia, the baby with her pink cheeks and big, dark eyes. How she loved them all!

Later that evening, when all the food had been eaten, the dishes washed and put away, and baby Sylvia was asleep in her crib, the rest of the family sat under the *vigas* of the long, deep porch that ran the length of the house. Papá and Mamá were in their rocking chairs holding hands. Elías softly strummed his guitar as Tía Sara and Cecilia sang in low voices an old song about a *paloma*, a white dove. "Cucurucucu, cucurucucu, cucurucucu." The younger children sat quietly for once, with sleepy eyes. The only other sounds were crickets chirping in the garden and the occasional croak of a frog in the canal across the road. Without the lights of a big city, the stars sparkled in the dark sky like diamonds a jeweler had strewn across a piece of black velvet. The smell of green things growing filled the air. A moth fluttered against the screen door, drawn to the pale light coming from the kitchen.

Cecilia felt so much love and contentment that tears welled up in her eyes. And she thought that maybe it would be impossible to ever leave such a wonderful home and family and go far away to a new world filled with strangers. If only one could keep things just the way they were forever and still have dreams come true.

Julio

"What's the matter with these lazy chickens? *¿Por qué no están poniendo las gallinas?* Why aren't they laying any eggs? I've found only two eggs since yesterday morning," Mamá complained as she entered the kitchen with her empty egg basket.

"Maybe they're sick," said Tía Sara.

"No, I checked most of them, and they look fine. I wonder if a fox is getting into the chicken coop at night. I'll have to tell José to leave the dogs out tonight," Mamá said. "The children will have oatmeal in the morning until we find out the problem with the hens."

Mamá put on her apron and set a large black cauldron on the wood stove.

"Roberto! Roberto!" she called out the kitchen window. "Bring me a bucket of water!" Roberto, Fito, and Elías were hoeing weeds in the garden in front of the house. "And bring it quickly!" she added.

Bringing water from the outside pump was a chore that all the children hated. It meant placing a bucket under a spout and pumping the handle with all their strength until water began to stream out into the bucket. They had to keep pumping until the bucket was full and then carry the heavy bucket into the house, invariably splashing themselves and their clothes along the way. Then Mamá would be angry because their clothes were wet and they had tracked muddy footprints on her clean kitchen floor.

"Why do I always have to bring in the water bucket?" Roberto complained as he lugged it into the kitchen. "*¿Por qué yo?* Fito never has to do it."

"You sure are complaining today, Roberto," said Tía Sara. "*En boca cerrada no entra mosca*. A fly doesn't enter a closed mouth."

"Ay, Tía, no flies are going to get in my mouth just because I'm talking," Roberto protested as he set down the bucket, being careful not to splash any water on the floor.

"You mind your manners, *niño*, and don't talk back to your aunt or you'll get the *chicote* for sure," said Mamá with a warning look. "And if you don't behave, you won't get to paper the outhouse with the others this afternoon."

"I'm sorry, Tía. *Lo siento,*" said Roberto. He didn't care so much about the sting of the *chicote*, but he didn't want to miss out on the fun of repapering the family outhouse.

All the children looked forward to this activity, held every July. The outhouse was a small wooden shed near the house, which took the place of an indoor toilet. The walls of the shed were papered with brightly colored pages torn from catalogs and old magazines and even papers the children brought home from school. Right now Mamá was boiling water to make the paste they would use to stick the pictures on the walls. She would add flour to the water and stir it until it formed a thick paste. The children would dip their brushes in the paste bucket and smear glue across the backs of their favorite pictures. Elías, Fito, and Roberto always papered one wall with pictures of horses, dogs, cars, tractors, and airplanes. The girls, Cecilia and Belia, preferred pictures of flowers and ladies' fashions. Cecilia would even cut out poems from old magazines her Aunt María would grudgingly give her, and she would read them to everyone as she pasted them on the walls.

"The glue is ready. Roberto, go get your brothers and sisters, and you can start cutting out pictures," Mamá ordered.

Soon Roberto, Cecilia, and the others were hard at work. "Our wall is prettier than yours," boasted Belia.

"Your wall is for sissies," taunted Fito, and he shook his paintbrush at his sister, splattering glue all over her face and dress.

"I'll show you who's a sissy!" Belia cried, throwing a large glob of paste on Fito. Soon all the children had entered the fray and emerged from the shed covered with white paste.

"You look like ghosts!" said Papá as he rode by on his horse. "You'd better take a swim in the canal and wash off before your mamá sees you."

Screaming with laughter, the children jumped into the irrigation canal with all their clothes on. They didn't have to worry about their shoes because no one wore shoes in the summer.

"When you are finished, dry off and come out to the barn. The first watermelons are ripe, and I picked a few good-lookers for you," Papá said.

Sure enough, the watermelons were red and sweet and a perfect treat after all their hard work. Papá would choose a firm round melon, cut a slice, and taste it. If it were sweet, he would cut thick slices for everyone. If the watermelon wasn't sweet, Papá would just toss it into a bucket for the pigs. Nothing was ever wasted on the farm.

Later that night as Cecilia lay in her bed, tired and sleepy from the day's activities, she thought about another summer treat that lay ahead—the Fourth of July dance just two days away. She would get to see Johnny! She knew she would because the Fourth of July dance was a big event, and everyone from Rincón to Hot Springs would be there. She stretched out on the cool cotton sheets as a warm breeze fluttered the gauzy pink curtains in the open window. She could hear the gentle chirping of crickets and the other soft sounds of the country night. These sounds and the thought of Johnny Tafoya lulled her into a deep and dreamy sleep.

Cecilia looked in the small mirror she had propped on the wooden dresser. Papá had made the dresser for her when she turned twelve. The dark brown eyes that looked back at her were lit up with excitement. Tonight was the Fourth of July dance. Tonight she would brush her hair till it shone and wear her prettiest dress. Tonight she would see Johnny! Maybe he would fall in love with her like young men did in the romantic stories she read in Tía María's magazines. Perhaps Johnny would walk across the dance floor and take her in his arms to twirl and sway to the music of violins and guitars. Maybe he would bring her punch in a crystal cup and lean close to her, hanging on her every word. And she would smile up at him and feel so proud to have the smartest, most handsome boy in town giving her all his attention. For he wouldn't dance with any other girl—not Belle, or Virginia, or anyone! Only her. Only Cecilia. It just had to be that way. It had to be because she had dreamed it just that way last night.

Cecilia looked in the mirror again. If only she weren't so pale, or if only Mamá would allow her to wear rouge like the ladies in the city.

"*¡No, señorita!*" Mamá said. "No respectable girl paints her face. No daughter of mine is going to behave in such an indecent way."

"But, Mamá—" Cecilia tried to argue.

"*Todo lo que entra por los ojos es superficial. Lo que cuenta es lo que sientes con el corazón,*" said Tía Sara. "It is not what is on the outside, but what is on the inside that counts—what you feel in your heart."

Cecilia pinched her cheeks, bringing a little color to them. She brushed out her long dark hair, thick and wavy from the braids she had worn all day. She would wear her hair loose tonight with a white ribbon tied around her head to keep the long strands from falling in her face as she danced. For surely she would dance tonight. Dance and dance and dance.

She opened a small bottle and poured a little of the liquid it held onto her palm. It was rose water, made by boiling rose petals in water. She dabbed this homemade cologne on her neck and rubbed the rest on her wrists. Fragrant rose essence filled the air. For the rest of her life, whenever Cecilia smelled roses, she would remember this night.

Cecilia stood up and pulled on her good white cotton

stockings. She rolled them over her long, thin legs and bound them above her knees with rubber garters cut from the inner tube of an old bicycle tire. She stepped into her soft white leather shoes with their pointed toes, white laces, and square heels. Finally, she slipped her dress over her head and smoothed it over her body. It was a beautiful dress, the most beautiful she had ever owned. Tía Sara had made it for her, sewing a little bit of it every night during the cold winter months. As if longing for spring, Tía Sara had chosen a pale green fabric and had spent hours embroidering pink and white flowers across the bodice. A white sash wrapped around the front and tied into a pretty bow at the back. Cecilia looked fresh and summery, the essence of youth and beauty. She couldn't help but feel a little pride as she craned to see herself in her small mirror. She knew it was a sin to be vain, but tonight was special. Surely God wouldn't mind if just for tonight she felt pretty.

"Cecilia, Ceciliaaaaa! Where are you, *mi hija*? We're ready to go!"

Cecilia heard Mamá's impatient voice. "*Ya vengo*, Mamá. I'm coming!" And Cecilia ran out to join the family already jostling for places in the farm wagon. Papá had laid a layer of fresh hay over the wagon bed, so Tía Sara and the children had a soft place to sit as the wagon bounced over the rough country road. Papá and Mamá sat up front, Mamá scorer, you're in trouble because he's supposed to be dist the ball to the other players.

Bobby did have nine assists and only one turnover, and scored 32 points, his career single-game high at Duke, which ironic that it should come in his last game and a losing one at that.

. . .

Bobby: I was lost. I didn't know what to do with myself. Other teams were going to be playing and I wasn't and that had never happened to me before. In four years of high school and three years of college, I had always been involved in the final game of the year.

Now, teams would be playing and I wouldn't. And some of the teams that would still be playing are teams we had beaten. It was a funny feeling.

As much as it hurt to lose, something good came out of it. It's hard to explain, but I felt closer to my teammates and to Coach K after losing this game than I did after we won the two consecutive national championships. I guess there's something about adversity bringing people closer together. That seemed to happen with us. That adversity and finality seemed to cement our relationship.

. . .

As I have said, Bobby's game is looking for the pass in the first half, then turning shooter in the second half, when the opposition is laying off him expecting him to pass, and if his team needs his offense. Against Cal, Duke needed his offense almost from the start, and in the end it wore him down and hurt Duke.

As the game ended, the TV camera caught Mike Krzyzewski on the sidelines applauding his players as they came off the floor. Another example of Coach K showing his class.

The TV camera caught a shot of Bobby, looking so dejected,

holding Sylvia, Papá driving the two horses. Cecilia felt proud of her family. Mamá and Tía Sara looked so beautiful with their dark hair piled on top of their heads. They both wore hand-crocheted shawls around their shoulders in case the night proved a little cool. Papá looked fine in his dark suit and black felt cowboy hat. His mustache was neatly trimmed and his boots brightly polished. The children's shiny, scrubbed faces glowed with excitement. They were going, not to dance, but to run wild with the other children outside the dance hall, playing tag, leap frog, and just generally having fun. Usually, the only places the children of the town got to see each other were at school or at church for Sunday mass, or *misa*.

At last they reached the dance hall next to San Isidro Church. San Isidro was the patron saint of farmers. He was the one the people of Derry prayed to when they needed rain for the crops, or when a pest was attacking the chile plants. The church hall was brightly lit for the Fourth of July and decorated with red, white, and blue garlands and bows. Tables covered with red tablecloths were laden with punch bowls and platters of *bizcochitos, empanadas,* and other delicacies of the region. Mamá, Tía Sara, and the other ladies of the parish had worked hard all week baking these treats. The men had tied red, white, and blue streamers across the ceiling of the hall. The people of Derry were proud of having deep roots in this part of the Southwest and were even prouder to be Americans. The Fourth of July was an important day for them, even though they lived in such an isolated area.

Belia, Fito, and Roberto ran off immediately to find their friends. Elías, carrying his guitar, joined the musicians setting up on the small platform at one end of the hall. Mamá and Tía Sara sat in wooden chairs that lined the walls, exchanging greetings with the other ladies. Papá and the other men stood outside the hall, smoking cigarettes and discussing cotton and chile prices. Cecilia stood for a moment, unsure of where to go or what to do. Where were her friends? Where were her cousins? Standing alone, she felt as if all eyes were on her.

Suddenly, in a whirl of skirts, ruffles, and ribbons, she was hugged and squeezed by her cousin Belle and Virginia Lara, Cecilia's best friend. Belle was the daughter of Mamá's brother, Tío Ben, and his wife Tía María. Belle had a younger sister named Clorinda, but everyone called her Clory. She was Belia's age. Virginia lived on the adjacent farm and had been Cecilia's best friend since they were five years old.

"Oh, your dress is beautiful! *¡Qué bonito!*" exclaimed Virginia.

"What about mine?" asked Belle. "My mamá ordered it specially from the Sears catalog."

"It's beautiful too," said Cecilia. She knew Belle always had to be the center of attention. Belle's parents owned the only general mercantile store in town. They were the wealthiest family, and their daughters were indulged in ways the other children could only dream of.

"I'm so happy to see you, Cecilia. Mamá hasn't let me visit you in so long. I've been helping her put up vegetables for days. I have so much to tell you! Have you heard about Chuchi Ogaz?" And the girls huddled together exchanging news and gossip, completely unaware of the pretty picture they made in their pastel summer dresses.

Soon the musicians had finished tuning up and began playing the first song of the evening, "*Jesusita en Chihuahua*." It was a rousing, rollicking polka, and soon the floor was filled with bouncing couples. Cecilia looked around furtively for Johnny Tafoya. Where was he? She hadn't seen him at all, and she couldn't possibly ask Belle or Virginia about him.

Cecilia's heart leaped into her throat as a group of people parted, and she saw Johnny standing near the door. He was just coming in with several friends. They looked so handsome in their dark suits and white shirts with bolo ties at the neck. They all wore cowboy boots. These young men were hardworking farmers' sons who did their share of breaking horses, plowing fields, and lifting heavy bales of cotton and hay. They stood awkwardly, obviously ill at ease. They were more comfortable riding horses than asking young ladies to dance.

Belle giggled. "Oh, look! All the boys are here. *¡Qué guapos están!* How handsome they all look!" Then she added, to Cecilia's dismay, "But I think Johnny Tafoya is the cutest one of all. I hope he asks me to dance."

Cecilia's heart fell. She knew her cousin only too well. Belle always got her way. That's how she had been brought up. If she decided she liked Johnny, she would do everything in her power to make him her *novio*, her boyfriend. And Belle was one of the prettiest girls in Derry. Everyone admired the dark curls hanging in spirals down her back. Belle spent hours in front of her mirror primping every day. Tonight she looked especially pretty and vivacious.

"Blessed Mother, *Virgencita*, please don't let Johnny like Belle better than me, please don't let Johnny like Belle better than me," Cecilia prayed silently, over and over.

"I think he's very handsome, but I would like to dance with Felix Otero. He's always so polite to me," said Virginia. "And he has the most beautiful brown eyes."

"Who do you like, Cecilia?" Belle asked coyly.

"*Nadie*. No one, really, no one," Cecilia lied. "I'm too busy to think about boys. I have too many chores to do. And besides, I have to read a lot of books this summer to get ready for the high school entrance exam."

"Oh, you! You've always got your nose in a book. Not me. I love to dance, and I'm going to have fun tonight!" Belle said as she tapped her dainty foot in its patent leather shoe in time to the music. She tossed her head of beautiful dark curls.

Belle smiled at the group of young men, and sure enough, one of them broke away and walked over to the girls. He made a small bow in front of Belle.

"*¿Gusta bailar?* Would you like to dance?" he asked her shyly.

Belle smiled prettily and, taking his arm, waltzed off to mingle with the other dancers.

Thank you, Virgencita. Johnny didn't ask her to dance first, Cecilia thought.

Soon Felix Otero came to claim Virginia for a dance, much to her delight. As the couple waltzed, Cecilia admired her best friend's dark brown braids bouncing as she twirled in the dance. Virginia looked so pretty tonight in her blue dress with matching blue ribbons in her hair.

"*Buenas noches*, Cecilia. Would you like to dance?" Cecilia looked up to see the smiling face of B. C. Apodaca. His real name was Blas Celedino because he had been born on February third, *el día de San Blas.*

"*Buenas noches*, B. C. Of course!" And Cecilia lost herself in the rhythms of the lovely waltz. Dance after dance, and still Johnny hadn't come to claim her. *Why?* She puzzled over this with real anguish. She and Johnny were in the same grade and were the smartest boy and girl in the whole school. They had read books together and worked on projects together all school year, and Johnny had seemed to like her in a special way. Could she have been wrong?

At that moment, Cecilia saw Belle flounce up to Johnny and say something. He laughed and led Belle onto the dance floor. Belle always got her way!

Tears welled up in Cecilia's eyes, and she blinked hard to keep them back. How embarrassing it would be for the whole town to see her crying like a child. She forced a smile on her face as she looked up at her dance partner.

As the evening grew later, Cecilia lost all hope of Johnny asking her to dance. In fact, he had hardly danced at all—just with Belle and his sister Cleofas. Could that mean that Belle was special to him? Cecilia walked slowly toward Mamá and Tía Sara. She would hold baby Sylvia for a while. Maybe then she would feel better.

Cecilia felt a light tap on her shoulder. She turned and almost gasped. Johnny was standing there, smiling at her!

"Will you dance with me?" he asked.

"*Sí,*" was all she could answer.

He led her in the last waltz of the night, the very last dance.

"It's good to see you again, Cecilia," he told her over the sound of the violins.

Cecilia could hardly speak. She couldn't seem to get her mind and tongue to work together.

"I...well...yes. It's good to see you again too," she managed to say.

"I'm sorry I didn't ask you to dance sooner, but I'm not really one for dancing," he said.

"I think you're a wonderful dancer," Cecilia said with sincerity. In fact, she thought everything about Johnny was wonderful.

"*Gracias.* Thanks. You know, my father and some of the men are building a big bonfire outside right now. And then they are going to shoot off fireworks," Johnny said. "Will you watch them with me?"

"Of course. *Seguro,*" Cecilia said. She could hardly believe her ears. Was this really happening? Was Johnny really asking her to watch the fireworks with him? This was the best Fourth of July fiesta ever! "Thank you, Blessed Mother," Cecilia whispered to herself.

The music ended, and they followed everyone out into the field in front of the church. Cecilia and Johnny stood side by side watching the beautiful colors explode in the dark sky. Sparkling bits floated down, like pieces of stars falling from the sky. Cecilia was so happy, she thought her heart would explode too. Everything was so perfect. Could it stay that way forever?

That night the family rode home in the wagon, each one happy in his own way. Elías had played his beloved guitar. Fito, Belia, and Roberto, heads nodding in sleep, were exhausted from all the games they had played with their friends. Tía Sara sang a Spanish lullaby to Sylvia. Mamá rested her head on Papá's shoulder. Her family had made her proud tonight, dressed in their best and on their best behavior.

Cecilia, wide awake, looked up at the stars. At that moment, a falling star shot across the black sky.

This truly was an enchanted evening!

CANDIES
SOFT DRINKS
& CIGARETTES
GROCERIES
&
MEATS
A.E. CARRERA
1936

Agosto

"I only found five eggs this morning," said Mamá crossly to Tía Sara. "Those lazy chickens just aren't laying. I can't seem to figure out why. *¿Por qué será?*"

"Maybe we should call in the *veterinario*, Dr. Silver, from Hatch," Tía Sara suggested.

"We can't afford the fee," said Mamá. "We have no money until we sell the cotton in the fall. We need the money from the sale of the chile to repay the bank loan. And if something happens to the chile crop, I don't know what we will do."

"Let's scramble the eggs with the asparagus the children found yesterday. That will make them go further. And I'll heat up some beans with *chile con leche,*" said Tía Sara.

"That's good. Everybody loves chile cooked in milk," said Mamá. "Still, though, I would like to know what's ailing those chickens."

The family ate the eggs with wild, sweet asparagus. Belia and Fito had walked the length of the irrigation canal, checking its banks for tender green shoots. They had filled a basket and brought it proudly to the kitchen. Roberto hadn't helped them at all. He seemed to have disappeared all morning, and Fito had had to do his chores. In fact, Roberto had been disappearing a lot lately.

After breakfast had been eaten, Cecilia heated water on the stove to wash the dishes.

"Belia, don't run off. *Quédate*. You need to help. You can wipe the table and dry the dishes," she told her little sister.

Pouting, Belia picked up a dishcloth made from a flour sack and began to wipe the table.

"Elías, come here, *hijo*," Mamá said to Elías before he could walk out to begin his work in the fields.

"Take this old dry bread and feed it to the pigs and chickens." She held out a pan of torn up bread slices.

"*Seguro*, sure, Mamá. And tonight I'm going to play you a new song I learned on my guitar—'Indita Mía,'" said Elías, cheerfully. He never whined about doing chores on the farm. He loved farm work—plowing, hoeing, planting, carpentry, and even chopping wood. He loved anything to do with the rich-smelling dark earth of the fields. He loved the animals—four horses, two cows, six pigs, dozens of chickens, three dogs, a half-dozen barn cats, and even a peacock that strutted proudly around Mamá's garden competing with the colors of the flowers. He loved them almost as much as he loved Isabel Lara, the sweet girl from Rincón he was sure he would one day marry.

What Elías didn't like was school. He hated having to sit still all day on an uncomfortable wooden bench in a room that was freezing in the winter and burning in the summer. Unlike Cecilia, Elías was not a reader. Reading and studying just interfered with the freedom he felt while working on the farm or riding Panky, his favorite horse, across the fields.

"Maybe the chickens will start to lay again if they eat some of your Tía María's old bread," Mamá said.

Elías left, and Mamá turned to Tía Sara and Cecilia. "I don't know why my sister-in-law sends all the stale, old bread from her store. Who does she think we are? Does she think we are starving to death? She knows I make my own bread every Friday, and the best bread in the valley, too," said Mamá proudly. She thought for a minute.

"That reminds me, Cecilia. I told your Tía María that you would go over after breakfast to clean her house," Mamá said.

Cecilia's heart fell. She had been hoping to finish her chores at home and squeeze in some time to read a little of

Sir Walter Scott's *Ivanhoe.* For days she had been lost in the world of brave knights and their fair ladies. She wondered why she couldn't have a romantic name like Rowena instead of plain, ordinary Cecilia. Then she had a second thought. Maybe Tía María would let her read some of the magazines she subscribed to when she was finished with her work.

"*Está bien, Mamá,*" Cecilia answered. "I'll work extra hard so my aunt will let me read a magazine or two."

"I don't know why María wastes good money on all those magazines. I think she does it just to show off. She never reads them—just piles them in boxes in the shed," said Mamá.

"*Dios le da pan al que no tiene dientes,*" Tía Sara said. "God gives bread to the toothless one. Poor Cecilia would love to receive those magazines every month, but we can't afford them. And our rich sister-in-law just tosses them in the shed instead of donating them to the school. *Ay, Dios, así es la vida.* That's just the way life is."

Cecilia mentally agreed with her aunt, although she kept silent. It wasn't seemly for a young girl to criticize an adult or an older relative like Tía María.

Tía María was very particular about her things. She took great pride in her possessions. Cecilia was only allowed to read the magazines in the shed, where they were stacked in boxes. She was never allowed to borrow them or take them home. In the winter, she would sit huddled in her shawl, turning the pages with mittened hands. In the summer the small shed was suffocatingly hot, and flies and gnats buzzed annoyingly around her eyes. But she didn't care. To Cecilia it was paradise—boxes and boxes of *Life, The Saturday Evening Post,* and her favorite, *National Geographic.*

Cecilia especially loved the gold-covered *National Geographic* magazines. The pictures of faraway places transported her beyond the steamy little shed to exciting worlds inhabited by strange, colorful people. Arab women with dark kohl around their eyes, African tribesmen with feather headdresses, and Alaskan natives wrapped in polar bear parkas. Pictures of brightly lit cities—Paris, Madrid, Rome—fascinated her. Oh, to have wings to fly away to all those wonderful places! Places with exotic names like Madagascar, Honolulu, Morocco, Ethiopia! Did they really exist beyond the purple and blue mountains of the Black Range that surrounded her valley? Cecilia would wonder what lay beyond Loma Parda, the high brown mountain she could see in the distance from the kitchen window. Would she ever be able to see any of these places for herself? She would devour page after page, guessing at words she didn't understand, fighting back her frustration at not being able to read and absorb everything at once.

Cecilia hung out her dishcloth to dry and ran across a

small field to the Derry General Mercantile Store owned and operated by Tío Ben and Tía María. The family, including their daughters Belle and Clory, lived in an attached house at the back of the store. Cecilia opened the door of the store, bell clanging above, and went in. As usual, the smells of spices, chile, fruits, and vegetables filled her nostrils. The bell attracted Tío Ben's attention. He came in from behind a gray curtain which separated the store from the kitchen of the house.

"*¡Buenos días, bonita!*" he said. "How about an apple or a banana to finish off breakfast?"

"*Muchas gracias,* Tío," said Cecilia, choosing a crisp red apple. She didn't bite into it, but slipped it into her pocket to munch on later as she read her beloved magazines.

Tío Ben was the exact opposite of his wife. He was a lot like Papá—jolly, kind, and generous to a fault. He was the constant despair of his frugal and stingy wife. Whereas Tía María would offer her nieces and nephews stale buns and broken candy, Tío Ben would give them entire chocolate bars and handfuls of bubble gum. And better yet, whenever he would drive his car all the way to Ciudad Juárez, 90 miles away, to buy Mexican spices, baskets, soap, and other goods for his store, he would bring back *pan dulce*—Mexican sweet bread—and little toys for each of his nieces and nephews, as well as his daughters.

Tío Ben had the only car in town, and also the only telephone. The telephone fascinated Cecilia. It hung on the wall, shiny and black, with a handle that had to be cranked. Tío Ben never charged anyone to use it, but Tía María made people pay a nickel when she was there.

"*Ay*, Cecilia. *Ya era tiempo*. It's about time you got here. I have a lot of work for you to do. Ven, come with me," said Tía María as she looked into the store from behind the curtain.

Cecilia often wondered why Belle and Clory didn't have to help clean the house. They usually sat around in their ruffled dresses, Clory playing with her dolls and Belle daydreaming or looking out the window to see if any boys walked by. Cecilia never saw either of her cousins reading even one of the wonderful magazines that came regularly to their house. She thought of Tía Sara's saying about people without teeth and giggled to herself.

Cecilia worked tirelessly washing the large mound of dirty dishes left over from breakfast, dusting furniture, shaking out carpets, washing Tío Ben's shirts by hand and hanging them on the line outside to dry. Tía María wanted everything done in a particular way. Cecilia had to hang the shirts by the tail, and the bed sheets and pillow cases had to be hung in such a way that folding them would be easy when taking them off the line.

For lunch, Tía María gave Cecilia a peanut butter sandwich. It was so delicious! Cecilia ate it slowly, savoring every bite. Her family never had peanut butter or cereal in boxes like Belle and Clory. Her family ate only what they could grow on the farm. Store-bought food was a luxury they were rarely allowed. After lunch, Cecilia swept the kitchen floor and brought in several buckets of water. Every time she finished a task, Tía María had another one for her to do. Finally all the work was done. The laundry was blowing in the breeze, the house was sparkling.

"Here is a quarter for your work. Now you may go sit in the shed and read, but be sure to leave all the magazines in the right order," Tía María said, feeling generous.

Cecilia took the quarter and curtsied the way Mamá had taught her. "*Muchas gracias.* Thank you very much," she told her aunt. Then she ran off to spend the rest of the afternoon in her version of heaven.

When Cecilia got home, there was still more work to be done.

"Cecilia, go fill this basket with corn. We need at least a dozen *elotes* for supper," Mamá ordered. "Then clean them and be sure to get as much silk off as you can."

Cecilia sighed and trudged off to the cornfield. She walked through the tall stalks, picking the ripest-looking, plumpest ears of corn. The tough leaves of the corn stalks scratched her bare legs and arms and made them itch. She carried the heavy basket to the steps leading to the house and sat down to clean the ears of corn. As she pulled off the green leaves and the strands of golden silk, the scent of fresh corn filled the air. It was the smell of the country, of fresh air and fertile ground, of green things being given up by the earth. It was a wonderful smell!

Cecilia had been cleaning corn since she was a child. She wasn't squeamish about the fat green caterpillars found in every ear. She simply plucked them out and tossed them to the chickens who ate them greedily. The chickens strutted about, clucking, asking for more. "You greedy things," Cecilia told them. "You're as bad as the pigs!"

She rinsed off the corn at the water pump and took it into the kitchen. By now she was exhausted. Maybe she could lie down and rest for just a little while.

"*Ándale*, Cecilia, I need you to wash these pans. They take up too much room on the counter." Mamá was not done with her yet. Cecilia looked at the dirty pans with a sinking feeling. Mamá had killed a chicken. She had dipped it in boiling water to loosen its feathers, and Belia had plucked off all the feathers. The pans were full of bits of feathers, entrails, and blood.

Ugh! thought Cecilia. *At least I didn't have to pluck the feathers.* She hated the feel of the limp chicken in her hands and the sticky feathers. She also felt sorry for the chicken and sometimes couldn't even eat it if she had been the one to pluck it. Cecilia put a kettle of water to heat on the stove and with a deep sigh, resignedly plunged her hands into the hot soapy water.

In the morning Mamá gathered all the children and announced, "I need to order new school shoes for you from the catalog."

Fito and Roberto groaned. "I hate to wear shoes," said Fito. "They always hurt!"

"Me, too. *Yo también*," agreed Roberto. "They pinch my toes."

"Well, you will be glad enough for your shoes and socks when you are walking to school in the snow this winter," said Mamá. "Now, stand on this paper and let me trace your feet. And don't fidget because I'll get it wrong, and your shoes will come in the wrong size."

Each child stepped on a square of brown wrapping paper that Mamá had placed on the kitchen floor. Then Mamá took a thick pencil and traced an outline of each child's feet. Later she would mail these paper outlines to the catalog company, and they would receive new sturdy leather shoes in the mail. Sometimes the shoes came too tight or too large, but they had to wear them all the same. It was always torture to break in new school shoes after running barefoot all summer.

August was a special month for Cecilia. Not only did it mark the last days of summer, but it was her birthday month as well. In just a few more days, Cecilia would turn fourteen. She could hardly believe it! She felt so grown up, and the three-year age difference between her and Belia suddenly seemed enormous.

Soon Cecilia and Elías would be starting eighth grade—only one more year until high school! Although Elías was one year older than Cecilia, he had been retained in the first grade, and the two were in the same grade. Elías had always been embarrassed about being held back, and no one ever mentioned it. He could have been a better student, but he didn't try. He knew exactly what he wanted out of life, and school simply didn't fit in. Elías wanted nothing more than to be a farmer like Papá and some day marry Isabel. In fact, there already existed between the two families an unspoken agreement that their children would marry when they came of age.

"I don't understand why you can't study even a little bit before a test," Cecilia often told him during the school year.

"I don't have time to study," he would reply. "I have to help Papá fix the gate on the chicken coop." Or, "I have to brush Panky." Or, "I have to take a load of hay to the cows."

There was always something Elías had to do that was more important than studying.

In fact, just this morning she and Elías had the same argument over again.

"*Hermano*, don't you want to learn new things? How can you be satisfied just doing the same things every day?" Cecilia asked him.

"Cecilia, *tú no entiendes*. You don't understand. I learn new things every day here on the farm. Yesterday, I learned to trim the hooves of the horses myself. Tío Santiago showed me how. He says I do it better than him now. And right now Papá is teaching me how to patch the holes in the barn roof. Tomorrow we're going to plow the land up by the orchard. If I didn't do all these things for Papá, he would have to pay someone to help him."

Cecilia had to agree with him on that point. Without Elías' valuable help, Papá would not be able to work the farm alone.

"But, *hermano*, at night when I'm studying, you could study with me. I could help you learn our lessons," she insisted.

"I'm too tired at night to read books and write essays," Elías answered. "Besides, our cousins, Leo and Raymundo, and all the other boys don't do their homework either. Why should I be different?"

"Well, I want to be different," Cecilia said. "I don't want

to be stuck on this farm for the rest of my life. Don't you want to see what's out there in the rest of the world?"

"Not really. *Hermanita*, you and I just don't have the same goals. I'm not good at schoolwork. But I am good at working the farm. Now let me get to my work. I have to dig a new irrigation trench." Elías put on his hat and left to do the backbreaking job of ditch digging.

Cecilia watched as her brother strode purposefully toward the tool shed. He really was a good son and brother. He worked tirelessly on the farm without complaining the way Fito and Beto did. What would Papá do without him?

Cecilia turned her thoughts to her birthday. She knew everyone would be especially nice and considerate to her that day. In fact, Mamá had established a tradition that the birthday child did not have to do any chores on his or her special day. Cecilia could already imagine herself under the cottonwood tree reading to her heart's content.

The night before Cecilia's birthday, Tía Sara, with Belia's help, baked an enormous chocolate cake. "We had to use the only four eggs we could find," Tía Sara said. "The chickens just haven't been laying as they should."

Belia licked chocolate from the spoon. "*Mmmm*, I love chocolate. Can't we eat the cake now?"

"No, *niña*, this is for our special supper for Cecilia's birthday tomorrow," admonished Tía Sara.

While they baked the cake, Mamá had been wrapping presents—a lace *mantilla* for Cecilia to wear on her head at mass and a bright green velvet ribbon for her hair. Belia had saved her pennies and bought Cecilia a new pencil for school and a chunky pink eraser at Tío Ben's store. Fito and Roberto had swept the store in return for two thick pads of writing paper. They knew this gift was exactly what their studious sister would like. Somehow, Roberto even had enough money to buy her a bag of peppermints.

"Don't you have a present for Cecilia?" Belia asked Elías when he stopped by the kitchen to sample the chocolate icing.

"*Seguro,* but it can't be wrapped," he replied mysteriously.

"It can't be wrapped? What kind of present is that?" asked Roberto, scraping the last of the icing from the bowl with his finger.

"Yes, what is it? What is it? Tell us!" demanded Belia.

"You'll see tomorrow," Elías said with a sly wink.

Cecilia was deep in sleep when something roused her. A noise? Voices? What was it?

The dawn was just breaking as Cecilia sat up in bed, remembering it was her birthday. The sound—it was guitar music, voices singing. Could it be...? Yes! She was being serenaded! Cecilia jumped out of bed and quickly pulled on her chenille robe. She ran a brush through her hair and hurried into the kitchen. Mamá and Tía Sara were already there.

"*¡Feliz cumpleaños, hija!*" said Mamá, hugging her tightly.

"Happy birthday, Cecilia!" said Tía Sara. "Now go out on the porch and greet your serenaders."

As soon as Cecilia stepped out on the porch, the group of musicians started to sing:

El día en que tú naciste
Nacieron todas las flores.
El día en que tú naciste
Cantaron los ruiseñores.

Ya viene amaneciendo,
Ya la luz del día nos vio.
Ya despierta, Cecilia mía,
Mira que ya amaneció.

The day that you were born
All the flowers were born, too.
The day that you were born
The nightingales sang to you.

Now the dawn is breaking.
We've been seen by the light of day.

Wake up, my dear Cecilia,
See the dawn of the new day.

As Cecilia heard the lovely sounds of *las mañanitas,* the old Mexican birthday song, tears welled up in her eyes. She saw Elías standing before her playing his guitar. Around him stood several young men from the town, some playing guitars, some just joining in the singing. And there in the middle of them all was Johnny Tafoya, singing to her on her birthday! This was Elías' mystery gift to his sister—the gift of his music and his love.

Septiembre

"*La flojera es madre de los atrazos,*" said Tía Sara as she roused Fito and Roberto at five in the morning on the first day of school. "Laziness is the mother of many troubles."

Fito and Roberto groaned and pulled the sheet over their heads.

"*Levántense.* Get up," Tía Sara said. "You have to do your chores before you go to school. *Quien mucho duerme, poco aprende.* He who sleeps much learns little."

Summer was over. The long, lazy days of going barefoot and swimming in the canal had ended. School! Fito and Roberto hated it. Now they would have to milk the cows, throw hay to the horses, feed the pigs and chickens, and bring in water all *before* school each day.

School! Cecilia woke up with excitement and a feeling of anticipation. She would wear her new navy-blue dress with white piping around the collar and a red bow at the neck. Mamá had ordered it from the catalog. Three dresses for a dollar. One was dark brown with a large white collar, and the other was gray with a drop waist and a pleated skirt. Cecilia would alternate these three dresses for the rest of the school year. She had a new pair of black leather boots that laced up to the ankle, three pairs of cotton stockings, a gray sweater, and a heavy coat for winter. These items comprised her entire school wardrobe. But she was fortunate. Belia had only hand-me-downs to wear. Cecilia's outgrown dresses were cut down to fit her by Tía Sara and refurbished with new bows and buttons.

School! Cecilia jumped out of bed and began to dress. She paid special attention to her appearance. After all, she was fourteen now. In another year she would be in high school—almost an adult! She brushed her dark hair until it was smooth and shiny. She slipped on her navy-blue sailor dress, white cotton stockings, and the new shoes. She spun around, admiring the swirl of her skirt. She wanted to look as pretty as possible on the first day of school because she would be seeing Johnny! She felt giddy with excitement. She knew the other girls in the eighth-grade class would all be wearing their best, especially Belle. Tía María had taken

Belle and Clory all the way to El Paso to buy new clothes for school. Belle had been bragging about her new dresses for days. Clory didn't have to wear hand-me-downs like Belia. Her parents could afford to buy her new clothes of her own.

School! Cecilia could hardly wait to start learning new and wonderful things. She wanted to know all about the rest of the world. She wanted to read everything that had ever been written. She had to make high grades this year—she just had to. At the end of the year, her class would take the high school entrance exam. Those who didn't pass would have to repeat the eighth grade or drop out altogether. She shuddered at the prospect of not passing. More than anything, she wanted to graduate from high school and get a job. She wanted to learn to use a typewriter and take shorthand, and to move to a big city like El Paso. When she graduated from high school, she could get a job and help Papá with the bills and the farm mortgage. All their troubles would be over, and maybe Papá wouldn't have that worried look she saw on his face when he was settling accounts each month. Maybe then Mamá and Papá wouldn't argue late into the night. Cecilia had heard them when they thought the children were asleep. She could hear their voices, Mamá saying angrily, "*Por Dios*, José, why do you give everything away? You need to start charging your friends for our chile, for our vegetables! You need to stop lending our tools to people who don't give them back! Your family should come first!"

And Cecilia would hear Papá say wearily, "Leave me alone, *mujer*. It's been a long day. *Déjame dormir*. Let me sleep."

Mamá and Papá never argued except about money, or the lack of it. Mamá's father, Grandfather Domenico Luchini, had been a wealthy man and had founded the town of Derry. He had owned many acres of land which he had received as a land grant from the United States government when he was discharged from the Union Army. But the land had been split among his ten children when he died, and now Cecilia's family lived and farmed Mamá's and Tía Sara's portion. It was barely enough to meet their needs. Yes, money was always a problem. But someday Cecilia would be smart enough and educated enough to help her family.

School! If Belia didn't wake up soon, she would be late!

"Belia, wake up! *¡Ándale! ¡Levántate!*" Cecilia insisted as she shook her sleepy sister. "We need to help Mamá with breakfast, and I don't want to be late to school—not on the first day!"

After breakfast, Elías led the quarter-of-a-mile walk to the one-room schoolhouse they all attended. Behind him walked Cecilia and Belle, and behind them followed Belia and Clory. Fito and Roberto, uncomfortable in their stiff new shoes, brought up the rear.

"How do you like my new dress?" asked Belle. "Papá drove us all the way to El Paso just to buy us our new school clothes." Cecilia had heard this many times before, but she answered good-naturedly, "Your dress is beautiful. That green color goes so well with your hair."

Belle patted her dark hair proudly. "I put curling papers in my hair last night. They were so uncomfortable that I didn't sleep a wink, but it was worth it. Aren't my curls beautiful?"

Thus went the conversation all the way to the schoolhouse. Once in the classroom, the students gathered in their own class section from first through eighth grade. This year, a total of thirty-six students were in attendance. One teacher taught all the students in all the grade levels.

Miss May Malone was already standing at her desk, ready to receive the children. She had been their teacher for two years, and they all loved her. She was kind and patient and even spoke a little Spanish. This helped put the little ones at ease, as many of them still didn't speak or understand English very well. Cecilia adored Miss Malone. She thought Miss Malone was the prettiest, smartest lady she had ever seen. In fact, she wanted to be just like her when she grew up—graceful, poised, and educated.

Cecilia and Belle went to sit in the eighth-grade section with the older students in the back of the room. The younger students sat near Miss Malone's desk. In the center of the room was a potbellied stove that kept the large room warm in the winter. The boys took turns chopping wood to keep it burning. If a student got sick, Miss Malone would place a quilt in front of the stove for the student to lie on. The room also contained several bookcases, a globe of the world, a blackboard, and a table with a pail and dipper on it. The pail and dipper were for drinking water. Each morning two students would carry the pail outside to the hand pump. They would fill the pail with water and carry it between them back to the schoolroom.

Cecilia and Belle greeted everyone joyfully. They hadn't seen some of their friends all summer. Some of them lived on distant farms and ranches and came into Derry only to attend school.

"*Buenos días*, Cecilia," said Johnny Tafoya, standing tall and neatly dressed before her.

"Good morning," said Cecilia, but before she could say anything more, Belle rushed over and interrupted.

"Oh, Johnny, you mean boy! You said you were going to visit me this summer, and you never did. And you only danced one dance with me at the Fourth of July dance," Belle pouted prettily.

"*Lo siento*. I'm sorry," said Johnny. "I had too much work to do on the farm, and I'm not a good dancer anyway."

"Well, you'd better make up for it at the next dance, or

I'll never speak to you again!" teased Belle.

Johnny laughed and took his seat. He turned and winked at Cecilia. She thought she would faint! He had winked at her as though they shared some secret, and Belle wasn't part of it. What did he mean by it? She was so absorbed in this enigma that she failed to hear Miss Malone's voice until Belle pinched her.

"Cecilia, would you and Belle bring in the pail of drinking water this morning?" Miss Malone was asking. It was an honor for the two girls to be asked on the first day of school. "And Fito Gonzales and Celso Bencomo can clean the blackboard after school," Miss Malone added.

Cecilia and Belle walked out to the pump. "I'll hold the pail, and you pump the handle," Belle ordered. Cecilia began to pump the handle up and down. Operating the handle was the hardest part of the chore. It took a lot of strength and effort, and Cecilia's arm began to get tired. Finally a trickle appeared, and then a stream of water began to flow into the pail.

"Be careful! You're splashing me!" cried Belle.

Distracted, Cecilia looked up at Belle and placed her other hand on the lid of the pump. The lid was loose, and Cecilia's index finger got caught between the lid and the pump.

"*¡Ay, ay, me corté el dedo!* I cut myself!" Cecilia cried as blood began to spurt from her finger.

"Oh, don't get blood on my dress!" cried Belle. "*¡Cuidado!* Hold your finger away!"

Cecilia began to feel the pain shooting through her finger and hand. Oh, how it hurt! She grew dizzy from the pain and from the sight of her blood. She bit her lip and tried to hold back the tears.

"Let's go back so Miss Malone can put a bandage on it," said Belle. The two girls walked quickly back into the schoolroom, Cecilia half supported by Belle. When she saw them Miss Malone cried, "Cecilia, my word, just look at you! Come here, child, and let me see."

Cecilia held out her finger and again felt like fainting, for the tip of her finger had been almost completely severed and was dangling at an angle.

"We must get you home now. Your parents need to take you to the doctor in Hatch and get that stitched up," said Miss Malone with concern as she wrapped a piece of clean white gauze around the wounded finger.

"Elías, walk your sister back home and tell your mother to take Cecilia to the doctor," ordered Miss Malone. She gave Cecilia a comforting hug and said, "Don't worry. Everything will be fine. Hurry along now."

Alone with Elías, Cecilia began to cry at last. The pain was unbearable.

"*Pobre hermanita,*" Elías said tenderly as he supported

his sister with his arm around her waist. "Don't worry. Remember how I cut my finger with the axe last Christmas? Dr. Steele stitched it up and it healed right away. It didn't even hurt," he added, trying to comfort her.

As he led her into the kitchen, crying and bloody, Mamá and Tía Sara jumped up from the table where they were shelling peas and cleaning beans.

"*¿Mi hija, qué te pasó?*" cried Mamá.

"What happened?" echoed Tía Sara.

"Cecilia caught her finger in the water pump," explained Elías.

"*Hijo*, run and get your papá. We need to get Cecilia to the doctor," said Mamá, immediately taking charge.

"I'll hitch the horses to the wagon, too!" said Elías as he ran out the door.

Dr. Steele, calm and efficient, stitched up Cecilia's finger and gave her some aspirin to lessen the pain. "Go home and put her to bed," he told Mamá. "She's had a bit of a shock. Keep her warm and give her plenty of fluids. No school today or tomorrow if she has too much pain."

No school! Cecilia began to cry again. She would fall behind in her classwork! She wouldn't see Johnny! And she had blood all over her new dress!

"Don't cry, *niña*, don't cry," crooned Mamá as she cuddled Cecilia in the wagon on the way home.

"But why did it have to be me? Why couldn't it happen to Belle?" Cecilia cried.

"*¿Qué culpa tiene San Pedro que San Pablo sea pelón?* What fault is it of Saint Peter that Saint Paul is bald?" said Tía Sara. "How is it Belle's fault you cut your finger? She's not to blame, and you should not wish ill on your cousin."

"But my dress! I've ruined it! And Belle has so many dresses!" sobbed Cecilia.

Mamá just hugged her closer and stroked her head. "Don't cry, *hijita*, don't cry," she crooned softly. Cecilia sniffled, enjoying the loving attention from her mother.

That night Tía Sara came into the bedroom Cecilia shared with Belia. Cecilia was lying in bed, her injured hand propped up on a pillow. She was groggy from exhaustion and pain. Mamá had made her a tea of *hierbabuena*, mint tea, sweetened with honey. Mamá said this would help her sleep.

"I have a surprise for you," said Tía Sara. She held out the navy-blue sailor dress with the white piping for Cecilia to see. No blood stains!

"Tía! It's perfect! Like new!" cried Cecilia gratefully. "How did you do it?"

"Oh, I have a lot of little tricks up my sleeve," said her aunt. "*Para todo hay remedio, menos la muerte.* There is a remedy for everything except dying, and don't ever forget it!"

Later that week Cecilia walked across the small field that separated her house from Belle's. She felt guilty about wishing ill on Belle, so she thought she would pay her a visit and show her how well her finger was healing.

"*Pásale, pásale,*" welcomed Belle. "Mamá just made some apricot *empanadas*. Let's have some with milk."

Although Tía María wasn't as good a cook as Mamá or Tía Sara, Cecilia ate the turnovers hungrily. The milk was frothy, cool, and fresh.

Later, as Cecilia was leaving, Tía María handed her a bag of old bread and some *empanadas* to take home.

"Here, *niña*, take this food to your mamá. I understand things haven't been going too well for your family lately," she told Cecilia.

Cecilia was confused. Their money problems were not any different than usual. And they always had plenty to eat. *Mamá will just feed the old bread to the chickens*, she thought. Aloud she said, "What do you mean, Tía? I don't understand."

"Well, I mean that Roberto has been selling me your eggs for weeks now. I assumed your papá and mamá needed the money," Tía María answered, gloating.

Cecilia stood rooted in place by shock and surprise. So that's where the eggs had been going! The chickens weren't lazy or sick after all! Roberto had been stealing them from the chicken coop early in the morning. No wonder he had been so willing to get up early, jumping out of bed before his brothers to get a head start on the chores. No wonder his pockets had been full of candy lately. He had said he'd been helping Tío Ben at the store.

Roberto! Cecilia managed to thank Tía María politely and then walked slowly home deep in thought. Mamá would be furious if she found out! Papá would probably laugh and think it was a great joke. Tía Sara would have an appropriate *dicho*. But Mamá would be absolutely angry and humiliated. What would she do to Roberto? Cecilia shuddered to think. She had to do something quickly. She had to punish Roberto in some way so he knew he had done wrong, and at the same time, preserve Mamá's pride. A smile began to creep across her face.

"I know what to do!" she exclaimed aloud. She had come up with a plan, but it would require the help and silence of Belia, Fito, and even Elías.

The next morning, all the children were up extra early, much to Mamá's surprise. They even went willingly outside to do the morning chores before school. Roberto dashed off shouting, "I'll feed the chickens!"

The others, barely controlling their laughter, sneaked up to the chicken coop and waited. As Roberto came out, he turned to latch the door behind him. Then they struck!

Cecilia, Elías, Belia, and Fito surrounded him and began to pummel him and squeeze him and press his overalls against his body. They could feel the crunch of the eggs he had hidden in his pockets as they smashed them with their hands.

"There! That's what you get," said Elías. "Don't ever steal our breakfast again! I'm sick of oatmeal!"

Roberto began to cry. "Ay, look what you did to me! I'm all wet and sticky!" His pockets were filled with broken eggs. The cloth of his overalls was already sticking to his body. The smell of raw eggs began to fill the air. He stuck his hands in his pockets and pulled out a gooey mess.

"I'm going to tell Mamá!" he started to wail. Then he realized he couldn't tell Mamá anything unless he admitted his crime. He'd get the *chicote* for sure!

"Jump in the canal and wash off," suggested Belia.

"He can't," said Fito. "Mamá will wonder why he's all wet. And he'll be late for school."

"You'll just have to wear your overalls all day until after school. Then you can wash in the canal," said Cecilia.

Sniffling all the way to school, Roberto cast angry glances at his brothers and sisters. They, on the other hand, laughed until their stomachs ached. All day Roberto sat in the hot schoolroom, his clothes sticky and smelly. All afternoon the other students kept complaining about the strange odor in the classroom, and Roberto's seatmate, Celso Bencomo, sat as far away from him as possible.

"You stink!—*¡Apestas!*" complained Celso. "Miss Malone, Roberto smells just awful!"

"Now, Celso, I'm sure the odor must be coming from something else. Maybe a mouse died under the floorboards. I'll hear no more about it. Concentrate on your work." And she gave Celso a very stern look. Roberto just sat red-faced and silent. He had never been so uncomfortable or so embarrassed in his life! Cecilia and Elías exchanged knowing glances. They knew they would all have eggs for breakfast in the morning!

Octubre

Cecilia breathed in deeply from the clear morning air as she walked through Mamá's garden. The fall flowers were in bloom—bright yellow chrysanthemums and deep red geraniums with their pungent scents. The waist-high zinnias in gold and orange were blooming their last multicolored petals. Cecilia hated to see them die. They were her favorites, but they would be back next summer. Most farmers' wives had only herb and vegetable gardens. But not Mamá. She had inherited her love of flowers from her own mother, Eusebia, and she had the most beautiful flower garden in the valley.

The smell of burning leaves wafted in the air. Elías and Papá must be burning the dead leaves and branches they had collected yesterday. Fall was Cecilia's favorite season; there was something bittersweet about it. The fields had given up their bounty of chile and cotton. The vegetables had been harvested and canned to be eaten over the long winter months. Jar after jar of pickles, peaches, apricots, tomatoes, okra, fava beans, sweet relish, jellies, jams, pickled onions and beets, and best of all, spicy hot jalapeño peppers filled the shelves of the *dispensa*. Cecilia especially loved the peaches canned with cloves. They were delicious!

For the last two months, Cecilia had been helping Mamá wash, peel, pare, slice, chop, pit, and cook fruits and vegetables. She would come home from school and work late into the night sterilizing jars and filling them with whatever vegetable or fruit they were canning before she could even begin her homework. But all the work was worth it when she looked proudly at the full shelves of their pantry and knew she had done her part in helping to feed the family. They wouldn't go hungry this winter.

Another smell filled her nostrils—a very familiar one in this Rio Grande valley. The spicy, tangy smell of green chiles laid out to turn red and dry in the sun. Mamá, with Cecilia's help, had washed the long green peppers and had spread them on large trays and on old window screens. Then Papá and Elías put them on the corrugated tin roof of the storage shed so they would be safe from ground insects and animals.

But the most beautiful things in Mamá's garden were the *ristras* of red chile peppers. Papá tied the green and red peppers into long, layered bundles and hung them from wooden frames. The *ristras* were left to dry where passers-by could see them and buy them. Papá was an expert at stringing *ristras* and often won a first-place ribbon at the county fair in Hillsboro. Mamá would get upset because Papá never charged enough for his *ristras* and many times just gave them away. For Cecilia, the bright red color of the drying chile was a reminder that Christmas was not too far away.

The cat's claw vine that grew on trellises along the porch was turning orange and gold. Cecilia felt intoxicated by all the regal colors around her. She stood looking toward the cotton fields and Loma Parda beyond them. She thought the fluffy white cotton balls looked like snow. October was cotton-picking time—some of the hardest work on the farm, yet the most important. The cotton crop brought the family the money they needed to make the mortgage payments and buy the necessities they could not grow or make themselves. Fabric, shoes, school books, sugar, salt, coal oil, and medicines were just some of the items the cash from the cotton sale would provide.

The last cutting of the alfalfa would be done as well. The cut alfalfa would be dried and bound in bales to feed the animals over the winter. After the cutting, Papá would let the cows and horses loose in the fields to finish eating what was left.

Cecilia met Tía Sara walking back to the house with a basket of apples.

"Come help me store these apples, Cecilia." Cecilia willingly followed her aunt into the *dispensa* where two large barrels of sand sat ready. Cecilia and Tía Sara wrapped each apple individually in pieces of old newspapers and buried them in the sand. This kept them from touching each other and rotting. The sand kept the apples cool and dry all winter. In a corner was another pile of sand where yams and potatoes were buried. Later during the winter, Mamá would ask one of the children to dig out potatoes for dinner.

"Don't forget Papá is taking all of you to the mountains today to gather piñon nuts," Mamá said as she carried in another basket of apples.

"Oh! I had forgotten!" exclaimed Cecilia. "Papá said we would camp out tonight and come back tomorrow."

"You need to dress warmly and take the heaviest blankets. It gets very cold up in those mountains," Mamá warned. "I don't want any of you getting sick. I have enough to worry about."

"*Hombre prevenido nunca será vencido*—always best to be prepared," added Tía Sara.

Mamá packed baskets with sandwiches, sweet buns, and apples. She packed bacon for Papá to fry in a big black iron skillet over the campfire for their breakfast. The children would drink hot coffee that Papá would perk on the fire. Mamá and Tía Sara were staying behind. They would enjoy their afternoon and night alone without having to cook meals and clean up after the children.

Papá and Elías hitched the horses to the wagon, stopping occasionally to rest and water the two horses. Finally, they came to the wooded area where they camped every year. Pine trees and piñon nuts were abundant. Enough pale daylight remained for them to start filling their baskets. They would gather more in the morning before heading for home.

"I'll make the fire. Cecilia, you can cook our supper. You can fry up the *chorizos* your mamá packed for us," Papá said. Cecilia unpacked the homemade sausages her mother had sent with them while Papá set up the coffee pot to perk the fragrant steaming coffee. This was one of the few times the children were allowed to drink coffee. They loved it heavily sweetened with sugar.

That night they sat around the campfire singing along to Elías' guitar. The three younger children were a little frightened of the dark and sat close to Papá, the firelight reflected in their eyes. They asked Papá to lead them in their favorite song, a song he had learned as a child, and he was happy to comply:

El elefante toca violín,

Toca guitarra, también pistón.

Y un camarón me dijo,

'¡Ay qué amigo tan panzón!'

Allá en los mares

Donde yo estaba

Cerca del agua

Cerca de un mes,

Habían peces

Tan delgaditos

Como la punta

De un alfiler.

¡Ay, cómo me asustaban!

Agua por Dios pedía.

Y un camarón me dijo,

'¡Eso sí que no hay aquí!'

The elephant plays the violin,

Plays the guitar, also the horn.

And a little shrimp told me,

'Isn't he the chubby one?'

There by the ocean
Where I was staying,
Beside the water
About a month,
Lived little fishies
So small and thin
Like the head of
A tiny pin.

Oh, how those fishies scared me!
I begged God to give me water.
And one little shrimp told me,
'That's one thing
We don't have here!'

"*Ándale*," said Papá after they finished several songs. "*Vámonos a dormir*. Let's get some sleep. I feel a chill in the air, so cover up well."

The children all slept in their clothes in the bed of the wagon, keeping warm from each other's body heat and the heavy blankets Mamá had packed for them. How exciting it was to sleep under the stars in the overwhelming serenity of the mountains! The wind in the trees whispered a lullaby to help them sleep.

In the morning, they awoke startled to find they were

covered by a fine powdery layer of snow. "It snowed! It snowed!" shouted Roberto, shaking snow out of his hair.

"I'm freezing!" said Belia. "And I'm covered with snow!"

"I'll get the fire going. You'll be warm in no time. I'll heat some water for you to wash your faces," said Papá.

Cecilia started frying the bacon and potatoes for their breakfast. The smell of bacon frying was incredibly delicious and made everyone's mouth water. The cold, snow-covered morning whetted the children's appetites.

"I'm starving!" cried Fito.

"Mmmm, that smells good," said Roberto.

They sat on blankets and ate their bacon and potatoes with flour tortillas Cecilia had warmed on the griddle. The coffee was perfect—hot and sweet.

"*¡Vámonos, niños!* Let's get started gathering nuts. We'll be leaving in a couple of hours," said Papá. "We don't want to get caught in any more snow."

All the way home, Cecilia and the others cracked the hard brown shells with their teeth and munched on the sweet white meat of the piñon nuts. Mamá would use them to make piñon brittle and other candies and cookies for Christmas. The piñon harvest was another sign that fall was here.

October was the first month the children bathed inside. The

weather was too cold for them to use the irrigation canals. Bathing inside was a Saturday night ritual. Mamá and Tía Sara heated pans and kettles of water to fill a large metal tub. Then the children took turns bathing in the tub. After every two or three children bathed, the tub would be dragged outside, emptied, and carried back into the kitchen and refilled with hot water. It was exhausting and back-breaking work.

Several years ago, Cecilia had insisted on bathing first while the water was clean. "*En esa agua no me voy a meter. ¡Yo quiero agua limpia!*" she had cried. "I won't get in the dirty water. I have to go first!" she had insisted. After that outburst, Mamá always let Cecilia be first, especially now that she was a young lady. She even gave Cecilia her own towel. The boys didn't care anyway. In fact, they didn't even want to bathe. They didn't mind being dirty.

After they bathed, Mamá gave them rose petal and sugar tea. The tea was part of the cleansing ritual. Mamá boiled rose petals in water, added sugar and poured it into a jar. She placed the jar in the irrigation ditch to cool in the water. The rose tea was sweet, cool and delicious. For the boys, it made up for having to take a bath.

Mamá and Cecilia had been washing clothes all morning. Cecilia was impatient to finish her work on this warm Saturday morning. She longed to lean against the old cottonwood tree and read the book on Greek mythology Miss Malone had lent her. It was full of fantastic stories of horses that could fly and gods who turned people into trees. Her favorite myth was the one about Pandora's box. Cecilia identified a little with Pandora. She knew how it felt to be so curious about something that she just couldn't stand it any longer.

Mamá usually did laundry on Mondays, but today was such a warm fall day that she knew the clothes would dry quickly on the clothesline. The cloudless blue sky meant there would be no risk of rain wetting the hanging clothes.

Washing clothing and bedding was one of the most labor-intensive chores on the farm. It was strenuous work, and afterwards every muscle in Cecilia's body ached. Doing laundry required more than one person because so much was involved in the process. First, logs of wood were arranged in a shallow pit in the ground against the canal levee, and a fire was started. Then a large metal grate attached to four legs was placed over the fire. A large heavy cast iron cauldron was placed on top of the grate, usually by Papá or Elías. Finally, bucket after bucket of water had to be pumped, carried and emptied into the big kettle. Today being Saturday, all the younger children had helped fill and carry the buckets. Once the water was boiling, Mamá put the clothes in along with her homemade soap and stirred them with a long wooden pole. Then she lifted out each piece with the pole and dropped it into another tub filled with clean cold water to rinse out the soap. That tub had to be emptied and refilled with clean water several times. What a chore! No wonder Mamá made the boys wear the same trousers all week. No wonder she became so angry when they got their clothes dirty playing in the hay or the mud. After the clothes were rinsed, they had to be wrung out by hand and hung on a clothesline to dry. Later, they would be taken down and ironed. But that was another chore and another day.

Finally all the week's clothing was washed, rinsed, wrung and hung out to dry.

"When the water has cooled, I'll have Papá empty the cauldron. Then you can help me roast chile on the hot coals," Mamá told Cecilia. "Go read your book, but make sure the children don't get near the fire."

"*Seguro*, Mamá. Of course," Cecilia said. Now she could get back to the ancient world of unpredictable quarreling gods, hideous monsters, and handsome heroes. She sat under the cottonwood tree and was vaguely aware of the boys' voices near the bridge that crossed the canal. She wasn't worried—they were far from the cauldron.

Thoroughly engrossed in her book, she didn't realize that Fito, Roberto, and their two visiting cousins had carried their cowboy and Indian game nearer the fire. They were on the levee of the canal, running back and forth, pushing and shoving each other. Reluctantly, Cecilia looked up from her imaginary world and realized the boys were playing roughly and too near the fire.

"*¡Niños, cuidado!* Go play somewhere else!" she shouted.

Just at that moment, Fito lost his footing and slid down the embankment of the canal on his back with his legs straight out before him. His left foot slid right through the hot metal grate and into the red-hot embers. Cecilia screamed as she ran to pull him out. The shouts of the children brought Mamá and Tía Sara running from the kitchen.

"*¿Dios mío, qué pasó?*" Mamá cried.

"What happened? Who got hurt?" asked Tía Sara, running behind her sister. It seemed as though everyone was shouting at once. Cecilia had pulled Fito from the embers, and he was wailing in pain. Mamá shouted to the other boys.

"Go get Papá! Tell him to hurry! *¡Apúrense!*"

Mamá reached Fito and immediately pulled off his leather shoe. Hot ashes had fallen into the shoe and severely burned his foot. As she pulled off the shoe, pieces of burned flesh came off too.

"*¡Ay, mi hijo! ¡Ay, mi hijo!*" Mamá kept crying.

"We must take him to Dr. Steele right away," said Tía Sara. "Cecilia, run to the store and tell Tío Ben we need him to drive Fito to Hatch. The wagon is too slow!"

Cecilia ran as fast as her long thin legs could carry her. She burst through the door of the general store and gasped the news to Tío Ben. Tía María came out from behind the curtain followed by Belle and Clory.

"*¡Ay, pobre Fito!*" they all cried when they heard. "Poor Fito!"

Tío Ben ran outside and cranked up his Model T Ford. He drove the short distance to Cecilia's house. Cecilia ran behind, her heart in her throat.

Pobre Fito. Poor Fito. It's all my fault. It's all my fault, she kept repeating in her mind. *It's all my fault!*

"*Ándule, niños*," said Tía Sara. "Come into the house and we will pray for Fito to get well."

The subdued children straggled inside and knelt on the hard wooden floor of the parlor in front of the niche that held the statue of the Blessed Mother. Tía Sara began praying. "*Bendita María*, Blessed Mary, please take away Fito's pain and make him well." Then she led the children in praying the rosary. They knelt before a small altar Mamá had set up in one corner of the parlor. The statue of the Blessed Mother was surrounded by candles and wax flowers. Cecilia, trembling with guilt and worry, turned her ashen face up to the statue of Mary.

"Please, *Virgencita*, make Fito well!" she prayed fervently.

That night Fito was put to bed with his bandaged foot propped on a pillow. Mamá had fed him chicken soup and crackers with butter. The children got store-bought crackers only when they were sick. Fito lay pale and whimpering while Mamá held his hand.

"Mamá, let me sit with Fito, please. *Por favor*, Mamá. I'll take care of him tonight. I'll give him water when he's thirsty," Cecilia begged.

Mamá had said nothing to Cecilia about the accident. But Cecilia, deep in her heart, felt she could have prevented Fito's accident if only she hadn't had her nose in that stupid book! She deserved for Mamá to whip her legs with the leather *chicote*. Exhausted from crying and worrying, Cecilia lay down next to Fito. She squeezed her eyes shut to hold back the tears, and before she knew it, she had dozed off. She was awakened by voices in the room. Mamá and Tía Sara were talking.

"Look at Cecilia, sound asleep. My poor daughter is exhausted. *Pobrecita*. I thought about punishing her for Fito's accident, but the poor girl is punishing herself. She is so upset, I'm worried about her. Cecilia is such a good girl. I love her dearly. In fact, she is the child closest to my heart, the daughter I always wanted. I just wish I could make her understand that her books are nothing but trouble," said Mamá. "I need to find a way to make her abandon this foolish dream of high school."

"But, *hermana*, listen to me. I have tried to keep out of your arguments with Cecilia. She is your daughter, not mine. But I look at her and see myself. Remember, I too had a dream."

"Sara, I know you did. I'm sorry our father was so unfair to you. I know how much you and Edmundo loved each other and how badly you wanted to marry him. Believe me, I cried into my pillow many nights in my sorrow over your heartbreak. I saw you like a pale ghost moving through the house with no life in your eyes after our papá refused to allow your marriage."

"*Ay,* Josefina, I know you did, and I always loved you for it. But there was nothing anyone could do. Not even our mamá could make him change his mind."

"Sara, I want you to know that I have always felt guilty that I was allowed to marry and that you have spent your life helping me raise my children," Mamá said.

"It's not your fault our father wouldn't accept Edmundo. He truly believed Edmundo was lazy and wouldn't work hard to give me a decent life. Perhaps he was right after all. Edmundo left for California, and I never heard from him again," said Tía Sara.

"*¡Ay, mi pobre hermana!* We love and need you, and you will always have a home here. What would we do without you?" asked Mamá,

The sisters embraced, and laughing, wiped each other's tears from their cheeks with their handkerchiefs.

Cecilia wondered if she was dreaming. She had never known that Tía Sara had had a dream and that her heart had been broken. Could it really be true that Tía Sara was not living a life she had chosen? Had she sacrificed herself for all of them? Cecilia felt confused and ungrateful. She had always taken Tía Sara's presence for granted. She tried to wake herself completely, but the soft voices of her mother and her aunt praying the rosary lulled her to sleep once again.

Sometime around midnight, Tía Sara tiptoed in, dressed in her nightgown with a shawl around her shoulders. The warm October day had turned into a chilly fall night.

"Cecilia, *niña*, go to your bed. I'll sit with Fito now," whispered Tía Sara.

"Oh, Tía!" sobbed Cecilia, and she threw her arms around her aunt. "It's all my fault! I should have been watching the boys. Instead, I was reading a book. I was selfish, and look what happened!" Cecilia cried.

Tía Sara hugged her niece tightly. "No, Cecilia, it is not your fault. What happened was God's will. It is not our place to question what God does. Go get some sleep.

Tomorrow you need to put on a smile for Fito and cheer him up," Tía Sara told her. "*Al mal tiempo hay que ponerle buena cara.* We have to be brave and strong in good times and in bad times. Tomorrow things will look better—you'll see."

Noviembre

Tía Sara was right. Things did look better in the morning. Even though Fito was in pain, he was enjoying all the attention he was getting. The children were never pampered and cosseted unless they were sick. To be served breakfast in bed was a rare luxury. Cecilia took Fito a tray with fried eggs, bacon and *refritos*—beans refried in bacon drippings. She treated him with a rolled-up flour tortilla spread with quince jelly made from the fruit he had helped pick last summer.

"Let me cut up your eggs for you, Fito. Are you comfortable? Do you need another pillow?" Cecilia asked, fussing over her brother. Everyone else had gone to Sunday mass, but she had insisted on being the one to stay behind with

Fito. A deep feeling of guilt still nagged at her. It felt like an elephant was sitting on her chest. Every time she looked at Fito's pale wan face, she relived the horror of the accident all over again.

"After I wash the breakfast dishes, I'll come back and read you a story from my mythology book," she promised him.

"*¡Sí, sí!* I want to hear all about the monster that was half man and half bull," Fito said with excitement.

"You mean the Minotaur," Cecilia explained. "Yes, I'll read to you all about him and how he fought with Theseus."

After Cecilia had heated water, washed all the dishes, dried them, put them back in the shelves, wiped the table, swept the kitchen floor and thrown out the dishwater in the garden, she dried her hands and went in search of her book.

"Fito, look at these beautiful pictures," she said as she sat in a chair next to the wrought iron bed where Fito lay. He sat up in bed, propped up by pillows with another pillow under his foot. When Mamá came back from *misa*, she would take the bandage off his foot, clean the burned skin, apply the salve Dr. Steele had given her and put on a clean bandage. She would have to do this every day for weeks. During all this time, Fito could not step on his foot. He would not be able to go to school or run and play with Roberto and his friends. Cecilia was determined to keep him from being bored. She would entertain him as best she could during whatever time she had free between school and her chores. She would put aside her beloved books until Fito was well.

Fito poured over the beautiful colored pictures of Pegasus, the flying horse, and Poseidon holding his trident.

"Oh, look at this!" he shouted, pointing to a page. "She's horrible! *¡Qué fea!*"

"That's Medusa. She had snakes for hair," explained Cecilia. "And anyone who looked at her would be turned to stone! But my favorite is the story of Pandora. I'll read that one now. Then I'll read a new myth to you every day," she promised.

The next Sunday, Tía Sara stayed home with Fito because Cecilia had to go to confession at the church before *misa*. Mamá insisted that everyone in the family go to confession every Sunday. Sometimes Cecilia had no sins to confess. She hadn't talked back to her mother, she hadn't been cross with her little brothers, and she hadn't had mean thoughts about her cousin Belle. She would agonize over what she was going to tell Padre Arteta until her stomach ached. Finally, she would resort to making up little sins just to have something to say. Then she would feel more guilty leaving the curtained booth than when she went in.

This Sunday, though, she really did have a sin to confess. She had waited anxiously all week to talk to Padre Arteta. She felt so much guilt and anxiety over Fito's accident that she could think of nothing else. She felt God was frowning on her for allowing such a terrible thing to happen to her brother. Cecilia wanted to confess everything to the priest and tell him how sorry she was.

"Bless me, Father, for I have sinned," she whispered in the confessional.

"*Dime, niña*. Tell me what is troubling you, Cecilia. You looked very worried when you came into the church," Padre Arteta said gently.

"*Ay*, Padre," Cecilia said with a sob in her throat. "I did a terrible thing. Just terrible. I'm a horrible person." She began to tell him of the Saturday afternoon when Fito burned his foot while she read a book. When she had finished, she was crying profusely into her handkerchief.

"Cecilia, your duty was to watch your little brothers. You made a mistake and the consequences were great, but they could have been worse. People are not perfect. We all make mistakes. But God is merciful, and he forgives us. If you are truly sorry, God has forgiven you already. Don't cry anymore, *niña*. Go kneel before the altar, and thank God for your blessings and say a rosary as your penance. And don't forget to take good care of your little brother." And with those comforting words, Padre Arteta slid shut the little window between them and turned to hear the confession of the penitent on the other side.

Cecilia felt a burden lift from her chest. The elephant was gone! She truly was sorry, so God must have forgiven her. In her relief, she knelt in a pew in front of the altar and said not one, but two rosaries.

That night she read Fito the story of King Midas and how his touch turned his daughter into gold. But Cecilia didn't need to read the story to learn what was of value in life and to appreciate the people she loved. She already knew that love is the most important thing of all.

November was the month when Papá and the boys went up into the mountain to cut wood for the winter. They took the wagon drawn by the two farm horses and spent several days finding fallen branches and cutting the logs to fit Mamá's kitchen stove. This stove would provide the only heat in the large house all winter. Cecilia and the others would get up on frosty winter mornings and carry their clothes to the kitchen where they would dress by the warmth of the stove.

Cecilia and Belia were not allowed to accompany the boys on the woodcutting trips. Woodcutting was serious business, and Papá didn't want to have to worry about the girls. So Cecilia stayed home and cleaned the coal oil lamps that lit the house at night.

"You're always staying up late reading and using the lamps, so you must be the one to clean them," Mamá would say. Cecilia would use a dry rag to wipe off the black soot from the glass *bombilla*. When she was finished, her hands and arms would be black up to the elbow. As she had to do this almost every day, her fingernails were always edged in black soot. Virginia had the same problem, and the two friends would commiserate over the sad state of their hands. They were envious of Belle, who never had to clean an oil lamp chimney.

"Petroleum jelly," Tía Sara advised. "Rub petroleum jelly into your cuticles and on your hands every night. And always sleep with gloves on. You will wake up with soft, white hands."

Cecilia always admired the hands of her cousin, Carmela Carrera. Carmela was three years older than Cecilia. She had been blinded at birth by an incompetent midwife who put the wrong drops in her eyes. Now she was a student at the School for the Blind in Alamogordo. Since she was blind, Carmela couldn't do the kind of chores Cecilia did. Instead, she sat inside out of the sun and the wind and crocheted or knitted. She also played the piano beautifully. Her hands were smooth, soft, and creamy white.

"Oh, Virginia! I forgot to tell you," Cecilia told her friend at school. "My cousin Carmela is coming to spend Thanksgiving with us. She promised to teach me how to crochet a lacy edge around my handkerchiefs."

"How fun! I want to learn, too," said Virginia. "Can I come over so she can teach me, too?"

"*Seguro.* Of course," said Cecilia. "Carmela would love to have you visit. I can hardly wait till she gets here. I haven't seen her in over a year. But I know she is still as beautiful as ever. I hope I can be as graceful and beautiful as she is someday."

"Me, too," agreed Virginia. Both girls idolized the lovely cousin with her slim, graceful figure. Carmela was Belle's cousin, too, but Belle was always jealous of her even though she was blind.

"Tío and Tía are bringing her to have Thanksgiving dinner with us. They are going to stay a whole week. Please come visit. Carmela will love for you to come, and she can show us the new crochet pattern together. We'll have such fun!" said Cecilia. "Did you know she's going to enter a convent next year?" she added.

"*¿De veras?* She's going to be a nun? How romantic!" Virginia sighed.

"Yes, she's going to devote her life to God. She's going to learn how to teach other blind children," explained Cecilia. "Everything is so special whenever Carmela comes to visit. Mamá loves her so. Every night we will get to sit in the *sala*, and Carmela will play the piano. Papá will play the violin and Elías his guitar. And we will all sing. We will have so much fun!"

Virginia listened wistfully. She came from a small, quiet family, and she didn't have a beautiful blind cousin who was going to be a nun.

The *sala* was only used on special occasions like Christmas or when entertaining visitors. Then Papá would make a big roaring fire in the parlor's corner fireplace, and Mamá would put her best lace tablecloth over the large round table that filled the center of the room. Mamá would serve *galletas* and coffee. The children would be given milk fresh from the cows to drink with their cookies.

"Will Carmela be here for the school Thanksgiving program?" asked Virginia.

"*Sí*. She won't be able to see it, of course, but she can hear it and imagine it," said Cecilia.

"You're so lucky. *¡Qué suerte!* You get to play Priscilla Mullins in the play," said Virginia.

"I know. I couldn't believe it when Miss Malone chose me!"

"Well, I only get to be a Pilgrim maid. I don't even get to speak," Virginia said.

"Yes, but your mamá made you the nicest costume. You are going to look so pretty!" Cecilia told her sincerely.

"It is pretty, isn't it?" agreed Virginia. "Mamá used material left over from one of her dresses. It's such a soft, silvery gray," she added.

"Mamá made Elías a black Pilgrim hat," Cecilia said. "And he made a beard out of sheep's wool. Poor Fito would have played an Indian, but he still can't stand on his foot. Papá is going to carry him to see the play."

The yearly Thanksgiving play was a big event at school and in the small community. All the mothers used their creative talents to make costumes for their children out of whatever scraps of material they had at home. Every student had a part in the program, either as a Pilgrim or as an Indian. In fact, the entire community became involved. There were costumes to make, lines to learn, scenery to build—everyone helped. Mamá and Tía Sara had been sewing costumes on the old Montgomery Ward sewing machine every night for weeks. Their legs ached from operating the foot pedal that drove the machine. Papá and Elías had helped build the wooden props of cabins and trees. The schoolroom would be converted into a Pilgrim settlement with a long banquet table. The entire cast would gather around it at the end of the play in a prayer of thanks.

"Have you seen Belle's costume?" asked Virginia.

"*Ay, sí.* It's beautiful. My Tía María sewed beads all over the front of her Indian dress," said Cecilia. Belle's costume was beautiful. She was to be an Indian maiden, and her dress was made of soft brown suede fabric with fringe around the short hem. Belle had worn it when she came to visit Cecilia the day before.

"Don't I look perfect?" she asked her cousin. She had braided her hair into two thick plaits that hung all the way down to her waist. She wore a beaded headband around her forehead. Her "buckskin" dress stopped at the knees, exposing her shapely, chubby legs.

"I can't wait for Johnny and the other boys to see me in this costume. Our school dresses are so long. We never get to show off our legs. I'll bet they can't take their eyes off me," Belle told Cecilia.

Cecilia didn't respond. She was afraid if she said anything, she would have to tell it to Padre Arteta next Sunday in confession.

The night of the play was cold and crisp—perfect fall weather. The stars seemed near enough to touch. Cecilia was especially proud of her family as they entered the schoolroom because Prima Carmela was with them. Carmela was definitely the prettiest girl there. All the young men eyed her longingly but kept their distance. They knew she was already spoken for—she was to enter a convent.

The audience took their places with excitement. As the bustle and noise finally quieted down, the curtains parted and the play began. Miles Standish, played by Johnny Tafoya, strode on stage in black boots and a black Pilgrim hat. He asked John Alden to speak to Priscilla Mullins on his behalf. When John Alden, played by B. C. Apodaca, approached her, Cecilia was trying to concentrate on her lines. But as she looked up into B. C.'s red freckly face, she almost laughed. As he spoke his lines, she mentally connected the freckles that were splattered across his cheeks and nose. She almost let out a giggle as she realized they formed a pattern quite similar to the constellation of Orion the Hunter! Suddenly, she became aware of B. C. staring at her with a frantic look on his face. Oh! He was waiting for her line!

"Speak for yourself, John Alden!" she shouted. The audience tittered at the abruptness with which she spoke the famous words, and Cecilia could feel herself blushing.

The rest of the play ran smoothly. Pilgrims and Indians spoke their lines flawlessly, and the audience sat spellbound. Too soon the play came to an end as the Pilgrims and their Indian friends said a prayer of thanks and sat down to partake of a fine meal.

Suddenly, Roberto, who was dressed as a Pilgrim, stepped forward and shouted:

"A long, long time ago when all this land was new,
Our fathers built this country for you and you and you!"

As he spoke the last line, he pointed a toy gun at the audience with every "you" he uttered. The audience roared with laughter. Papá laughed along with everyone, but Mamá sat silent and tightlipped. Miss Malone, standing in the wings, quickly pulled the curtain closed as the audience applauded and people stamped their feet and whistled. The applause and laughter went on and on. Everyone thought Roberto's comical performance was part of the show. But Mamá knew it wasn't, and Roberto would have to be punished.

That night at home she gave him a choice: three swats with the *chicote* or three rosaries on his knees before the statue of the Blessed Mother. Roberto chose the swats. After all, they were over right away with a little stinging afterwards. But three rosaries! That would take all night!

Once the punishment was administered, Roberto was allowed to join everyone in the *sala* for *torta de chocolate* to celebrate the evening's performance and Prima Carmela's visit. Cecilia was excited to see her cousin again. Cecilia had always looked up to her and admired her beauty, her poise, and her many accomplishments. The two girls sat together on the sofa.

"Cecilia, I'll be entering the Sisters of Loretto order this spring. I've been accepted as a novice!" Carmela told her.

"Oh, Carmela, I'm so happy for you!" Cecilia said as she took Carmela's soft white hand in her own. Wondering about something, Cecilia asked her cousin shyly, "Carmela, have you always wanted to be a nun or...?" Her voice trailed off. Carmela understood what Cecilia was trying to ask.

"*Sí, siempre.* Always," said Carmela. "Becoming a nun has always been my life's dream. I know people think I am entering a convent because of my blindness. They think I can't do anything else with my life. But they are wrong. I know I can do anything I want. I can read Braille, I can play the piano, I can sew—I can take care of myself."

"Oh, I know you can," Cecilia said. "And it's wonderful that you are going to become a teacher. I just wondered if being a nun is what you really wanted."

"I can be a teacher without becoming a nun," Carmela explained. "But I have always felt a deep connection to God, and I believe I can serve Him best as a nun. He gave me the blessing of my musical talent. I want to thank Him by sharing my music with others. I want to teach young children to love music the way I do." She took Cecilia's face in her hands. Cecilia felt as if Carmela could see deep into her soul.

"Becoming a nun has always been my dream, my one goal in life. Now that I have been accepted by the Sisters of Loretto, I am happier than I have ever been," Carmela assured Cecilia.

"Oh, Carmela! I have a dream too!" Cecilia told her. "I want to go to high school and get a job in the city."

"Then you must never let go of that dream. You must work hard to make it come true. It's up to you," Carmela said, holding Cecilia's hand.

"But Mamá doesn't understand. She wants me to stay here and live on a farm and be like her!"

"If you have enough faith in yourself, Cecilia, you can see your dream become real. Faith in yourself and in God. Pray to Him, and He will answer," Carmela said, her face glowing with happiness.

"*Gracias*, Carmela, *gracias*. I will have faith. I won't ever give up," Cecilia promised.

Later, Carmela played the piano while the children danced around the room. Papá bounced baby Sylvia on his knee, chanting a rhyme from his own childhood:

Ya los enanos ya se enojaron
Porque las nanas los pellizcaron.

Now the little dwarves are angry
Because their nannies pinched them.

As Papá sang, he winked conspiratorially at Roberto. His feisty young son had shown his independent spirit tonight and reminded him of himself when he was a boy.

"*De tal palo, tal astilla,*" as Tía Sara often said. "Like father, like son."

Diciembre

Winter days on the farm were cold and short. Every day the sun shone weakly, casting a pale light over the empty fields. The spidery limbs of the fruit trees were bare of leaves, and the pecan trees held only a few stubborn unopened pods near their tops. Every day the wind blew sharp and cold. Cecilia had to button her coat all the way to the collar and wrap a knitted scarf around her head as she walked to school, struggling against the wind. Belia trailed behind, walking in the shelter of her older sister's form. The boys trudged reluctantly to school, hands in pockets, heads down to protect their newly washed faces from the wind.

"*Ay, tengo frío*. I'm so cold!" complained Belia through chattering teeth.

"At least you didn't have to go outside and feed the animals at five o'clock this morning," Elías said. The boys had been up since dawn, throwing hay to the horses and milking the cows. Elías had knocked the ice from the water pump as Roberto poured water over it to loosen the frozen handle. Their fingers were blue by the time they came inside for breakfast. Even Fito had helped by scattering dried corn for the chickens. His foot was much better now, and he could walk again, although with a slight limp. The days of being pampered were over.

Cecilia was relieved and happy to see Fito out of his bed and walking to school again. The Blessed Mother had answered her prayers. Every night before she slept for the last month, Cecilia had prayed the rosary. And she had made a special prayer to *San Judas*, the patron saint of hopeless causes. Every Sunday she had lit a candle to *San Isidro*, the patron saint of farmers and of their church. She knelt in prayer so long that Mamá and Tía Sara wondered if she would become a nun like Prima Carmela.

"Cecilia, wait! *¡Espéranos!*" Cecilia heard a voice carried on the wind and turned around. Belle and Clory were running toward her. They were so bundled up in woolen coats, scarves, and mittens, they could hardly run. Cecilia and Belia waited for their cousins to catch up while the boys went ahead. They weren't interested in girl talk, and they wanted to get to school and out of the cold wind. They hoped Miss Malone had gotten there early and lit the wood stove. Then the room would be toasty warm, and they could huddle around the stove, warming their hands and faces.

Belle slipped her arm through Cecilia's as they trudged forward against the wind.

"Cecilia, you're invited to a *fiesta* at my house! A Christmas party!"

"*¿Una fiesta?* A party?" asked Belia, overhearing. "Can I come, too?"

"Yes, and the boys, too. Everyone is invited. Mamá said Clory and I could invite all our friends. I'm going to announce it today at school. Isn't it wonderful?" Belle said. Not waiting for an answer, she went on. "We're going to have a *piñata* and dancing, and best of all, Papá is going to make taffy, and we're going to have a taffy pull. You'll come, of course?"

"*Seguro que sí,*" Cecilia assured her. "I know it will be wonderful! Can I do anything to help?"

"Just don't hog Johnny Tafoya all to yourself. Give some of us other girls a chance to dance with him," Belle teased her cousin, giving her a sly look.

"Don't be silly!" Cecilia almost shouted. She kept her face down as though protecting it from the wind because she could feel herself blushing. "Johnny doesn't pay attention to me."

"Oh, yes he does. Everybody can tell you like each other," Belle insisted.

Cecilia felt panic rising in her chest at the thought that everyone, including Belle, had been discussing her and Johnny. How embarrassing! And what if Johnny heard about it? He would think she had told people she liked him. Oh, how awful! She had to fight the impulse to turn and run for home. Did everyone know she liked Johnny? Was it that obvious? Did they think she was a boy chaser? How could she walk into the schoolroom?

"*Ándale,*" said Belle. "It's too cold. Can't you walk faster?" She pulled Cecilia forward, their arms still linked. As they entered the schoolroom, Cecilia felt that all eyes were on her. The group of students huddled around the stove must be whispering about her. Miss Malone smiled at her. Did she know, too? It was all just too horrible!

Cecilia slipped into her seat, looking down at her papers, trying to hide her blushing cheeks. She was aware that Johnny had taken his place behind her, but dared not turn around to see if he was looking at her.

"Please rise for the Pledge of Allegiance," ordered Miss Malone. The class rose and recited the Pledge in unison. "Thank you. You may be seated. We will begin with reading today. Please take out your readers. Your assignments are on the chalkboard. Belle, please bring your book up to my desk and read orally to me," said Miss Malone. Belle flounced to the front of the room, and Cecilia buried her face in her book. She dared not look up, lest she catch Belle's eye. Belle might say or do something to further embarrass her.

The rest of the day was a nightmare for Cecilia as she avoided speaking to or even looking at Johnny. At lunch, she ate her burrito with Virginia at their desks, but couldn't bring herself to share her problem with her friend. When she got home in the afternoon, she ran to her bed and finally let loose the tears she had been holding in all day.

"*¿Qué te pasa, niña?*" asked Tía Sara when she found Cecilia lying on her bed.

"*Ay*, Tía, I'm just tired. I'll be all right. I've been studying too hard," Cecilia answered. She sat up and began to dry her tears with her handkerchief. Tía Sara didn't believe her for a moment, but was too wise to pry.

"*Los duelos con pan son menos.* It's easier to face your troubles on a full stomach. Come to the kitchen, and I'll give you a fresh warm tortilla with butter. And I made an apricot pie for supper from the apricots you helped me can in the summer." The thought of warm tortillas with homemade butter made Cecilia feel better. As usual, Tía Sara was right.

"*Sí*, Tía. Let me wash my face first. I'll be right there."

At the supper table, the conversation centered around Belle's invitation to the Christmas *fiesta*.

"It's about time María and Ben invited us to something," complained Mamá. "They eat here almost every Sunday and hardly ever return the favor."

"That's the way our *cuñada* has always behaved," sighed Tía Sara. "Her parents spoiled her, just as she spoils her own daughters."

"I wish I could be spoiled," said Belia wistfully.

"You're spoiled already—like a rotten tomato!" said Roberto.

Everybody laughed, even Belia. What would they do without mischievous, comical Roberto to keep them laughing?

At school the next day, Miss Malone told the class, "It's your job to decorate our Christmas tree." Two of the men from Derry had gone into the mountains to cut down a beautiful pine tree for the school. It stood tall and fragrant in a corner of the room. Its bare branches brought out the creativity in the students. They took Miss Malone at her word and worked diligently all week making Christmas decorations. They wound red and green paper chains around the tree and hung hand-painted ornaments cut from tin can lids. Dried macaroni was dyed with food coloring, strung on thread and draped around the branches. Belia, with Tía Sara's help, made a corncob angel to adorn the top of the tree. The dried cornhusks were twisted into wings. The angel's golden hair was made from silk embroidery thread. The tree looked beautiful, and everyone felt proud because each one had helped to make it so.

Decorating the tree had taken Cecilia's mind off Johnny for a while. But Belle's party was in a few days, and Cecilia would have to pretend that Johnny didn't mean anything more to her than B. C. Apodaca, Celso Bencomo, or any of the other boys she had grown up with. Still, on the night of the party, Cecilia dressed with special care because, after all, Johnny would be there. She wore her best dress and tied her shiny dark hair with the green ribbon Mamá had given her for her birthday. Her cheeks were flushed with excitement and anticipation. She was determined to have a good time. It wasn't every day the town had a *piñata* and a taffy pull.

Belle's house was filled with people when Cecilia and her family walked across the dry field that separated their house from Belle's. Tío Ben had oil lamps and candles burning throughout the house. A fire blazed in the fireplace of the *sala*. Evergreen branches decorating the room released their piney scent into the warm air. Belle and Clory had hung mistletoe and homemade decorations on the walls, over the doorways, and across the windows. An enormous bowl of cherry cider sat on a table surrounded by platters of *tamales*, sliced ham, potato salad, *frijoles, arroz, salsa*, homemade pickles, buns, and spiced peaches. Roberto immediately made a beeline for the watermelon rind pickled in molasses. Fito eyed the desserts hungrily. There were piles of round *buñuelos*. The crispy fried cakes were sprinkled with sugar and cinnamon. There were *empanadas* stuffed with plum and apricot jam and an enormous *torta de chocolate*, thick with frosting. Mmmm! Roberto furtively sneaked two *empanadas* into his pants pockets.

"*¡Niños, niños!*" cried Tío Ben. "*Vénganse*. Come pull some taffy!"

Squeals of delight filled the air as everyone raced toward the table where Tío Ben had placed trays coated with butter. He poured big blobs of hot melted sugar caramel on the trays. The children spread butter on their hands and grabbed handfuls of the soft candy. They began to pull and stretch the candy over and over until it lightened in color to almost white. Then they braided or twisted it into different shapes. The candy would be eaten warm and chewy or left to harden and then sucked on like a lollipop.

"Pull this with me, Cecilia," said a masculine voice. Cecilia looked up right into Johnny Tafoya's brown eyes. He held out a large lump of soft taffy. They pulled and twisted, fingers touching occasionally, until the candy began to cool and harden. Johnny's nimble fingers took the long twist of candy and began to shape it on a tray. He turned it deftly this way, then that way and stepped aside so Cecilia could see. He had shaped the taffy into a heart. Cecilia almost gasped. Was Johnny trying to say he liked her, or was it just an easy shape to make?

"Let's let it get hard. Then we can split it and each take a half," he told her.

"The *piñata*! The *piñata*!" shouted Clory. The men had hung the star-shaped *piñata* outside from a tree. The children were lining up, ready to be blindfolded to take a swing at the *piñata* with a wooden baseball bat. As each child swung, Tío Ben pulled a rope that lifted the *piñata* to safety. He would not allow the *piñata* to be broken until every child had had a chance to swing the bat. Finally, the last child swung hard and cracked open the clay pot inside the papier-mâché star. A shower of bright foil-wrapped candies rained upon the children as they scrambled to grab their share. Baby Sylvia screamed with delight in Mamá's arms. She clapped her chubby hands in excitement.

After the *piñata* had been broken, people began to say

their goodbyes. Cecilia and her family hugged and kissed their cousins and began their short walk home.

"Cecilia! Cecilia, wait!" Johnny shouted, running to catch up with her. In his hand he held the taffy heart. He broke it in half, right down the middle. "Here is your half," he said, holding it out to her.

"*Gracias*. Thank you, Johnny," Cecilia said, taking it. Johnny smiled and took a bite out of his piece. But Cecilia knew she would never eat hers. She would save it forever.

This Christmas turned out to be special in another way. For the first time, Cecilia's family had a Christmas tree in the *sala*. Papá was always too busy on the farm to go into the mountains just to cut a tree to decorate. But this year, on the last day of school before Christmas vacation, Fito and Roberto were helping Miss Malone clean the chalkboard and clear out the ashes from the stove.

"Boys, can you take the Christmas tree out and leave it on the trash pile behind the school?" Miss Malone asked.

Fito and Roberto looked at each other. They immediately knew what they were going to do. They each took an end of the bare tree and carried it home. Feeling very proud and clever, they set the tree up in the *sala*. Cecilia and Belia were delighted because now they would get to decorate the tree again. This time, they made popcorn balls glued together with molasses and hung them on the tree. Tía Sara gave them scraps of ribbon, and Belia tied them into bows. Mamá even gave Cecilia a dime to buy red-and-white-striped peppermint candy canes at Tío Ben's store. They hung these all around the tree. Then they stood back to admire their work.

"*¡Qué bello!* It's beautiful!" they all agreed as the pungent smell of pine filled the room. Now they would have a tree to put their little gifts under on Christmas Eve.

Christmas Eve was a festive time, filled with rituals and tradition. As soon as the cold winter night fell, the children ran indoors to wash their faces and change into clean clothes. Tonight they would be attending midnight mass at the *Iglesia de San Isidro*. Everyone went to *la misa de gallo*, even Sylvia.

They all gathered in the kitchen for a traditional Christmas Eve supper of *tamales*, homemade by Mamá. Cecilia and Belia had helped make the *tamales* by spreading thick *masa* onto clean, dried corn husks. Mamá filled the dough with tender pork and red chile. The *tamales* had been steaming for hours in a huge pot on the wood stove. The aroma had made the children's mouths water all afternoon. Now it was time to eat them! Of course, they all thought Mamá made the best *tamales* in the valley.

"I ate five *tamales!*" bragged Fito.

"So what? I ate seven!" said Elías, poking his little brother in the ribs and making him laugh.

"*Ya basta, niños,*" said Mamá. "*Dejen de jugar.* Quit playing and get ready for *misa.*"

The children bundled themselves in their warm coats and woolen scarves. Papá lit a kerosene lantern and hung it on a pole. Mamá gathered everyone together, and the family began the two-mile walk to the church. Papá held the lantern high to light their way over the rough country road.

Midnight mass was special, and the whole town looked forward to it all year. For the children, it was a rare treat to be allowed to stay up until after midnight. For their parents, it was a time of great devotion and a chance to celebrate the true spirit of Christmas. For Cecilia, it was an especially joyous occasion. She loved the warmth and comfort of the brightly lit church, and the beauty and serenity of the nativity scene the ladies of the church set up every Christmas.

Padre Arteta began the mass which usually lasted over two hours. But the children didn't mind. They were too excited by the novelty of staying up late and the prospect of special treats when they returned to the house.

After mass, the family gathered once again around the kitchen table to drink Tía Sara's thick, rich hot chocolate.

Cecilia curved her frozen fingers around the warm mug and breathed deeply, allowing the steam to warm her lungs. The children were hungry again after their cold walk. They snacked on *bizcochos* and *buñuelos*, traditional Christmas pastries.

"*Ahora a la cama.* To bed, all of you," ordered Mamá. This time the children obeyed eagerly. They couldn't wait for morning to see what surprises lay in store for them.

The first one awake on Christmas morning was Roberto. His shouts woke up the others as he found a stocking hanging at the foot of his wrought iron bed.

"Look what I got!" he cried, holding up a bright red metal truck.

"And look at this! Look at this! I got an airplane—just like the Wright Brothers' airplane!" said Fito.

Belia scrambled to the foot of her bed to find a new doll in her stocking—a beautiful store-bought doll, not hand-made like all her others. Cecilia was thrilled with her Christmas present. It was a book she had been wanting, A *Girl of the Limberlost*. Mamá had remembered!

"*¡Feliz Navidad, mis hijos!*" said Papá as he hugged and kissed each one.

"*Vénganse a almorzar,*" said Mamá. "Breakfast is ready."

After a hearty breakfast of *chorizo con huevos* and *tortillas*, Cecilia helped Mamá and Tía Sara clear the table and clean the kitchen. Christmas dinner had to be prepared.

Fito, Belia, and Roberto dressed warmly and spent the morning running to the neighboring farms, shouting "*Mis crismes, mis crismes!*" Their neighbors gave them little bags with nuts or an orange, a special treat in the winter. Mamá handed out popcorn balls made with molasses to the children who came to her door shouting the same greeting.

Soon Tío Santiago, his wife, and their sons Leo and Raymundo came to visit and stay for dinner. Tío Ben, Tía María, Belle, and Clory came as well. It was a tradition for all of them to celebrate Christmas at Cecilia's house, as it had always been the family homestead.

All morning Mamá roasted chickens and guinea hens in the oven, basting them with their sizzling juices every fifteen minutes. Tía Sara and their two sisters-in-law helped prepare the elaborate meal while they chatted and laughed like young girls.

"*¡Ya está la comida!*" Mamá announced at last.

"Lunch is ready! Lunch is ready!" shouted the boys as they ran from room to room. Soon everyone was seated in the dining room at the long narrow table that was used only for special occasions. Mamá and Tía Sara carried in platters of crispy golden hens surrounded by roasted onions and potatoes swimming in rich brown gravy. Everyone clapped and cheered. Mamá's face, already rosy from the heat in the kitchen, grew redder, but Cecilia knew her mother took great pride in her kitchen skills.

The children feasted until they thought their stomachs would burst. Afterwards, they sat in the *sala*, too full to move, and listened to Elías play the guitar while Cecilia and the girls sang "*Noche de Paz*" and other Christmas songs.

That night as she lay in bed, warm and cozy in her flannel nightgown, Cecilia thought about the day and how happy her family had been. They had celebrated Christmas together with plenty to eat and presents for everyone. She knew Mamá had scrimped and saved all year to buy her children something special for Christmas. But what touched Cecilia's heart the most was that Mamá had chosen a book as a gift for her. Perhaps Mamá was beginning to understand how important books and school were to her. Perhaps Mamá would let her go to high school after all.

Enero

The new year swept in on a blizzard of sleet and snow. On New Year's Day, the fields lay under a clean white blanket which muffled all sound. Only the occasional cawing of a black bird perched on a chinaberry tree broke the stillness.

Papá and the boys made giant footprints in the pristine snow as they trudged through the drifts on their way to the horse corral.

"Elías, make sure the horses are all right. Throw them some extra hay and make sure their water isn't frozen. Fito and Roberto, come with me," Papá ordered. He led them to the cow pen and sat them down to milk the impatient cows.

The cows mooed gratefully when they saw the boys coming. The boys were late getting to their chores on this frigid January morning, and the cows were uncomfortable and needed milking. Papá, with the farm dogs following and frolicking behind in the snow, made the rounds of the chicken coop, the barn, and other outlying structures to check on wind or snow damage. Luckily, everything appeared to be undisturbed. He cleared a drift from the chicken coop door and threw some dried corn to the chickens. Normally, the chickens would have been allowed to wander the farmyard freely, but today he kept them penned up. The snow was too deep for them to peck the ground.

"*Muchachos, ya está el almuerzo.* Breakfast is ready!" shouted Mamá from the kitchen window. Quickly finishing their chores, the boys ran as fast as they could through the snow, Papá following behind carrying two pails of milk. Some of the cream was already floating on the top. The children fought over who would get to skim the tops and eat the cream, but Papá made sure to get a dollop for his coffee.

In the warm kitchen, Cecilia and Belia were setting the table and pouring hot coffee into thick white mugs for their parents and Tía Sara. Baby Sylvia was in her high chair banging a spoon. She was hungry for her oatmeal.

"*Muchachas*, today you must help me do some mending. It is too cold to be outside, so you can mend the clothes, sheets, and pillow cases," Mamá said.

Belia groaned, but Cecilia didn't mind the mending and sewing. She liked to sit and make tiny stitches while she thought about a book she had been reading. She enjoyed making up stories in her head, which later she would recite to the younger ones at bedtime. Sometimes, as she sewed, she thought about the future and all the possibilities that lay ahead for her. Cecilia's mind was always busy. Besides, she and Belia sat in the cozy kitchen by the stove and were warm all day while the boys were outside clearing snow and breaking ice from the pump and the water troughs. Papá and Elías would even have to climb on the roof and sweep off the snow. The roof of the adobe house was made of large wooden beams called *vigas*, and was covered with plaster. Clearing the snow off would keep the roof from leaking or sagging.

"*Mañana* all of you will take your castor oil," Mamá reminded them. The children immediately began to protest and make groaning sounds. Roberto fell on the floor clutching his stomach, pretending to be sick.

"Get up, silly boy," said Mamá crossly. "You know you have to drink castor oil to start the new year right." The thought of the nasty-tasting castor oil almost ruined breakfast for the boys. But they knew they wouldn't be given much to eat the next day, so they finished off all the beans, tortillas, and oatmeal. After breakfast, Cecilia and Belia settled down to mend clothing from a large basket Mamá placed before them.

"Your eyes are younger than mine and your Tía's. You can see to thread a needle. That is why this is your job," Mamá explained. Cecilia wondered how they could not see to thread a needle. She could do it so easily! Deftly, she guided the white thread through the eye of a needle and picked up a shirt with a torn sleeve. Belia, with the gray cat in her lap, was mending a hole in a handkerchief. The cat kept pawing at her thread as she pulled it in and out of the fabric.

"Paloma, if you don't leave my thread alone, I'm going to put you out," Belia chided the cat. Paloma kept swatting the thread playfully, but Belia didn't follow through with her threat. Instead, she giggled and caressed Paloma's soft furry body.

Mamá brought another basket filled with handkerchiefs, aprons, bloomers, and pillow cases that had holes or ripped seams. These items were all made of sugar and flour sack material. Cecilia and Belia were not embarrassed by their bloomers, or underwear, because all the other girls wore the same fabric. Everyone bought sugar and flour in large cotton sacks. The sacks were carefully split open, and the resulting rectangle of fabric was put to many uses. Only outer clothing was made from store-bought fabric or ordered from a catalog.

Cecilia's needle moved expertly as she thought about her New Year's resolutions. *I'm going to try to read more,* she promised herself. *I'll try to do my chores more quickly, so I'll have more time to study. And I need to learn more words in English. I'll ask Miss Malone for a list of high school words. Then I'll try to learn three new words a day!* she resolved.

As she sewed, she also pondered how to get Elías to study with her. His grades hadn't been very good lately, and there was a strong possibility that he would not pass the high school entrance exam. And hadn't Mamá hinted that she would not let him be embarrassed by Cecilia advancing to high school while he was held back again?

"*Ay, Dios.* What am I going to do?" she sighed aloud.

"What did you say?" asked Belia, trying to keep Paloma from tangling her thread.

"*Nada, nada.* I'm just dreaming out loud," Cecilia said.

In the morning, Mamá made every member of the family line up in the kitchen—even Papá—and gave each a tablespoon of castor oil to swallow. Roberto tried to run away and hide, but Mamá grabbed the *chicote* and chased him as far as the chicken coop. Under the threat of a whipping, he trudged back to the house to face the nasty-tasting medicine.

"This will clean you out for the new year ahead," said Mamá.

The rest of the day, the children were given only crackers and the juice from the pot of beans. They had only rose water to drink. All day they took turns running to the outhouse in the cold.

"When I grow up, I'm never taking castor oil," declared Roberto. "*¡Nunca!*"

"Me either," said Fito and Belia at the same time.

"I don't know about that," said Elías. "Look at Papá. Mamá still makes *him* drink it!"

Three days later, a terrible thunderstorm blew in while Papá was in Hillsboro, the county seat, on business. That morning the family had awakened to a beautiful rainbow in the sky. "*Arco iris al amanecer, agua al anochecer,*" predicted Tía Sara as she too left to spend a few days with a cousin in Hot Springs. "A rainbow in the morning means rain in the evening."

Mamá was alone with the children when lightning flashed in the sky followed by loud peals of thunder. Sylvia began to cry in fear, and no one was able to distract her. The dogs howled and barked outside and made so much noise that Elías had to put them in the barn.

"I'll check on the cows too," he said.

"Be careful, *mi hijo*," Mamá cautioned. "*Cuídate.*"

"*No se apure,* Mamá. Nothing will happen. I can take care of things until Papá returns," Elías said as he ran out into the storm.

Papá! Cecilia's mother thought about her husband, caught by the storm on his way home from Hillsboro. He was returning by bus, but would have to walk over a mile from the public road to the farm. He would be drenched by the time he got home, or worse. What if a tree limb fell on him? Or he stumbled in the wind and injured himself?

"*San Cristóbal*, please watch over my husband," Mamá prayed under her breath to the patron saint of travelers. She didn't want to alarm the children. But she caught Cecilia's strained look and knew she also was thinking of Papá out in the storm.

The storm continued to rage. Mamá worried about the roof holding up or one of the animals getting hit by lightning. What if lightning came through a window? Mamá and Cecilia went through the house, making sure the windows were latched tightly and drawing the curtains over them. Mamá, superstitious as ever, covered every mirror in the house with a cloth. She, like the other townspeople, believed that mirrors attracted lightning.

"Stay away from the windows and the mirrors," she ordered the terrified children as thunder boomed over their heads. Belia covered her ears with her hands. Roberto wrapped himself up in a blanket. Sylvia was whimpering with fright. Mamá knew she had to do something to keep the children's minds occupied. They would pray! She went to the *sala* and returned with dry palm leaves she had saved from Palm Sunday last year. She placed pieces of palm leaf on a tin plate and lit them on fire with a match. As the palm leaves burned, she made the children kneel in front of the tiny fire, and then she led them in prayer.

"*Dios mío*, please protect us from this terrible storm. We beg you to keep us safe, to keep our house safe, to keep our animals safe, and to keep Papá from harm," she prayed.

"Amen!" they all answered.

Then she lit a candle for each child to carry and led them on a procession through the dark house from room to room. In each room was a *nicho*, or niche in a wall. Within this *nicho* was a *santo*, a statue of a saint. Small votive candles sat before each saint. As they went from room to room and saint to saint, Mamá lit each candle while they all knelt in prayer. Cecilia couldn't help thinking that the *Santo Niño de Atocha,* dressed in his oversized robes and peculiar hat, looked like a Japanese emperor, and she repressed a giggle. Then she was overcome with remorse and knew she would have to confess this to Padre Arteta next Sunday.

Cecilia's favorite *santo* was the one in her own bedroom, *Santa Cecilia*. She was the patron saint of music, and Cecilia was named for her. Maybe that's why Cecilia loved to sing so much. She liked to whistle too, but Mamá said polite young ladies didn't whistle and made her stop. Belia's favorite saint was Saint Francis of Assisi. Like Saint Francis, Belia loved all animals.

As the frightened family sat in the kitchen drinking hot milk, a loud peal of thunder shook the room. Belia screamed, and Sylvia began to wail. At that moment, the kitchen door flew open and there stood Papá, soaked to the skin! His legs were covered with mud from his shoes to his knees, and his face was streaked with dirt. But he was home, safe and sound, and stood with a big smile on his face, arms outstretched.

Everyone seemed to move at once. They ran into his open arms.

"¡Papá! You're home!" they all cried as they took turns hugging him.

"*Sí, hijos. ¿Qué creían?* What did you think? That a little storm was going to keep me from getting home to my family?" he joked.

Cecilia and Mamá looked at each other with relief. Who cared if the roof leaked or the garden was flooded? Papá was home!

Later that night, Cecilia sat huddled in her bed, fingers numb with cold. She read the book Mamá had given her for Christmas by the light of a coal oil lamp and underlined all the words she didn't know with a thick pencil Elías had sharpened for her with his pocketknife. She would look up the words in a dictionary when she returned to school and try to memorize them.

Cecilia felt a kinship with Elnora, the backwoods heroine of the book whose mother jeered at her desire to go to high school. The mother felt her country daughter would look foolish among the more prosperous townspeople. But Elnora knew that hard work, self-reliance, and a positive atittude could bring success. Discovering she could catch and sell moths and butterflies, she was able to pay for her school clothes, tuition, and books. Elnora graduated from high school and changed her life. If only things would end as happily for Cecilia as they did for Elnora, the girl of the Limberlost.

Belia loved the Christmas gift Mamá had chosen for her. Mamá had ordered the doll from the Montgomery Ward catalog. She and Tía Sara had been shelling pecans all fall and had sold the nuts for cash to buy special Christmas gifts for the children. There had been some years when the children had received only an orange and a few candies in a bag. But this year, the pecan trees had yielded a bumper crop. Mamá had splurged on a beautiful porcelain doll for Belia. The delicate features of the doll's face were hand-painted. Red curls like fat sausages adorned her head. She wore a blue satin dress trimmed with ivory lace and black patent leather shoes. Mamá and Tía Sara had shelled a lot of pecans to pay for this doll.

"I'm going to name her Rosalinda because of her beautiful red hair," announced Belia, tossing back her own long dark braids.

"Rosalinda. That's perfect," agreed Tía Sara. "We must have a baptism for Rosalinda."

Cecilia and Belia squealed with delight. A doll baptism! They would invite Belia's friends for refreshments, and they would all bring their own dolls. But first Padre Arteta would have to baptize and bless Rosalinda at the church.

A doll baptism was a serious occasion in Derry. When a girl received a new doll, the doll was taken to the *Iglesia de San Isidro* for the priest to baptize after mass. To prepare for this special event, Tía Sara began work on a new dress for Rosalinda. The baptismal dress was cut from silk fabric left over from Tía Sara's own first communion dress that she had worn so many years ago. Tía Sara spent evening after evening sewing ribbons and tiny pearl buttons onto the dress by the light of a coal oil lamp. Cecilia sat at the same table doing her homework by the same light. Light was a precious resource and couldn't be wasted. When she finished the dress, Tía Sara held it up for all to see.

"*¡Qué bello!*" cried Belia. "Rosalinda will look so beautiful! *¡Gracias, Tía!*" she said, hugging her aunt.

Mamá was busy making *molletes*, sweet buns flavored with anise, and *empanadas* filled with peach preserves. Belia cut paper into lacy doilies to use as placemats when her friends would come to eat the pastries and drink hot chocolate after the baptism.

Belia was the first one up Sunday morning. Today was her day! She braided her long dark hair into two plaits that hung down her back and then dressed Rosalinda carefully in her new baptism gown.

"*¡Qué bonita eres!* How beautiful you are! Rosalinda, you are the prettiest doll I've ever had!"

After mass, Padre Arteta waited at the altar with great seriousness for all the little girls to come forward and witness Rosalinda's baptism. It was a very solemn ceremony. Belia handed the doll to him, and he held it over the wooden baptismal font. He dipped his fingers into the holy water and sprinkling a few drops over the doll's head, he announced, "I baptize you María Rosalinda, in the name of the Father, and of the Son, and of the Holy Spirit. Amen."

Everyone repeated "Amen." He placed Rosalinda into Belia's waiting arms.

"Take good care of Rosalinda," Padre Arteta told her. "She was given to you in love."

"*Gracias*, Padre. I will," Belia answered solemnly.

All the girls raced back to Belia's house, carrying their own dolls in their arms. The *sala* was ready with a fire blazing in the grate and a table laden with pastries. The paper doilies looked elegant on the round oak table. The girls sat around the table, and Mamá brought out her special crystal pitcher filled with hot chocolate.

"Here, *niñas*," Mamá said. "Eat plenty and drink plenty because, *gracias a Dios*, today we have plenty." The girls said grace and began to stuff themselves with the delicious food and talk about their dolls. Everyone admired Rosalinda and her beautiful dress. Belia even allowed all of them to take turns holding her. It wasn't every day a beautiful doll like Rosalinda was seen in the valley.

Cecilia smiled at the younger girls and remembered her own doll baptism just a few years ago. Now she was too old for dolls. She was old enough to go to high school and study important and difficult subjects. All she needed was to pass that test—and pray that Elías would pass it, too!

Febrero

"Look in the mirror and you'll see someone I love." Cecilia read the words over and over again on the slightly crumpled sheet of paper she held in her hand. She had discovered the note in her arithmetic book. Someone must have put it there at school when she wasn't looking. She sighed.

"*Ay, Dios mío*. Who could have put this in my book? Was it really meant for me?" she wondered aloud. Maybe there was a mistake. Maybe someone got the wrong book, or maybe Belle was playing one of her pranks. And then another thought crept into her mind. *Could it be from Johnny?*

"Cecilia! Cecilia!" Belia was calling. "Mamá needs you in the kitchen. She wants you to make the *sopa*."

Cecilia quickly slipped the note in her secret hiding place—a narrow space behind the drawer in her little dressing table. No one, not even Belia, knew of the secret space. It was the one little bit of privacy Cecilia had in a house filled with people.

"I'd better get my mind on the *sopa de fideo* instead of love notes," Cecilia told herself. "If I burn the *sopa*, Mamá will kill me!" But February was the month of love and romance. *El Día de San Valentín* would be here soon, and everyone at school was already excited about giving and receiving valentines.

February was also the start of the plowing season. The fields had to be prepared for the spring planting. Plowing was the most arduous work on the farm. Papá, with Elías' help, did the plowing. Some years, if there was a little extra money, Papá would hire on a helper. But money was short this year, and they had to plow all the fields themselves. No one in the valley was wealthy enough to own a tractor. Every farmer still used a horse-drawn plow that was heavy and difficult to maneuver. The pointed tip of the plow dug up the furrows as the horse dragged it across the ground. Churning under the dry chile and cotton plants, Papá had to guide the plow so that the horse dragged it in a straight line. It took all day just to plow a small area of the frozen ground. Elías was so busy helping Papá every day after school and on weekends that Cecilia worried about his schoolwork. He never had time to study or do his homework.

"If only I could help with the plowing," she lamented, "I could take over for Elías, but I'm not strong enough." She knew that even if she were strong enough, Mamá would never allow it. Plowing was man's work. Cecilia's work was in the house. Cecilia and Belia were allowed, however, to help with the vegetable and flower garden in front of the house. Today they were covered up against the wind and sun with homemade bonnets on their heads. They worked stooped over in the garden pulling up dead plants and weeds. These would be hauled away by the boys to the mulch pile behind the barn.

"Cecilia, pick a nice cabbage for supper!" Mamá called from the kitchen door.

"*Sí,* Mamá," Cecilia answered. She searched for a tight green head of winter cabbage.

"I hope Mamá fries it with *manteca*," said Belia. "That's my favorite way to eat cabbage."

"Silly, Mamá *always* fries it in lard," Cecilia said, her back sore from stooping.

"Well, it's still my favorite," Belia insisted. "And I'm hungry. *Tengo mucho hambre.*"

"I hope she's making vegetable soup. I would love some hot *caldo* after this cold work," said Cecilia.

"Mmmm, that would be good too. I'm so hungry, I could even eat the cabbage raw," said Belia.

"Here, rinse the cabbage and take it to the kitchen," Cecilia said as she continued to pluck out weeds and dry stalks of dead flowers. The garden was a sad sight in the winter. But later this month, Mamá would have them plant seeds of all kinds of flowers and vegetables, and by May it would be a riot of color. Cecilia looked ruefully at her dirt-covered hands and broken nails.

There isn't enough petroleum jelly in the world to help these hands, she thought. *I know vanity is a sin, but why can't I have pretty hands like Prima Carmela?* Then she felt ashamed because Carmela was blind and would probably give anything to trade places with Cecilia. "Well, here's a sin I need to confess on Sunday," she muttered as she straightened her aching back.

"*¡Vénganse a la cena!*" Tía Sara called out. "Supper is ready!" The boys were already washing up at the pump. Cecilia placed her hands under the frigid flow of water, trying not to think of her rough chapped skin.

In the kitchen, Cecilia thought Mamá and Tía Sara were behaving strangely. They were whispering conspiratorially, even giggling. When they saw Cecilia, Mamá slipped something into her apron pocket, and they quickly returned to their kitchen duties. They seemed to be embarrassed at being caught acting in a lighthearted way.

"*¿Qué pasa, Mamá?*" Cecilia asked, genuinely curious. "*¿Por qué se ríen?* Is something funny?" She wondered if the baby had performed a cute antic.

"*No, no, hijita. No es nada,*" said Mamá, actually blushing.

"Josefina, show your daughter. She should see what a romantic man her father is," said Tía Sara, laughing.

Blushing even more, Mamá pulled out a card from her apron pocket and held it for Cecilia to see. It was a lovely little card covered with pink and blue flowers. In the middle of the card was a red heart with white lovebirds on either side. It was a valentine! Papá had given Mamá a valentine!

"*¡Qué bello!* How beautiful! Did Papá give it to you?" Cecilia asked.

"*Sí, hijita,*" Mamá said, turning back to her cooking so that Cecilia wouldn't see the smile on her face.

Cecilia had never seen Mamá behave in this way—like a young girl. Cecilia had never really thought about it before, but now she realized Papá and Mamá must be in love!

Supper that evening was delicious. Perhaps it was delicious because they were all so hungry from working in the cold all afternoon. Or perhaps it was so delicious because Mamá was happy. The cabbage was indeed fried in *manteca*. It was crisp and chewy, just the way Belia liked it. Even the usual beans and chile tasted especially good. And Tía

Sara had made fresh *tortillas de harina.* Cecilia used her flour tortilla to scoop up beans mixed with chile that had been simmered in fresh milk. *¡Qué sabroso!* She washed it down with a glass of milk from their own cows.

Winter had been dark and cold. Anything that could break the tedium of the short days and long nights was welcomed. As the only holiday between Christmas and Easter, Valentine's Day was enormously popular at school. It meant red construction paper, white paper doilies, and sticky paste on everybody's fingers. Miss Malone had collected empty cigar boxes from Tío Ben's store. She gave each student a box and announced: "We will have a contest to choose the best decorated box. The winner will receive this!" She held up a beautiful fountain pen. Murmurs of appreciation rippled through the room. No one could afford a pen like that. Everyone wrote with thick blunt-pointed pencils.

"I'm going to win that pen," announced Belle. "No one here has my artistic talent." Elías and B. C. snickered.

"What do you *campesinos* know? You're just a bunch of country bumpkins," Belle said as she tossed her hair over her shoulder.

All week the students worked on decorating their cigar boxes and making valentines for each other. On Valentine's Day, they would go from box to box, placing their cards into them. The overflowing boxes would be taken home and the valentine messages read and reread, providing hours of entertainment on these cold February nights.

Cecilia wanted only one valentine this year—one from Johnny. She furtively watched him as he folded red paper and wrote messages inside. When he finally had a large pile on his desk, he began working on one more. It was much larger than the others, and Johnny seemed to take extra care in decorating it.

"Who could he be making it for?" Virginia whispered. She too had noticed Johnny's intent absorption in his work.

"Maybe it's for his mother," Cecilia suggested.

"I don't think so," said Virginia. "It must be for a girl. Maybe one of us!"

Johnny frowned in concentration as he wrote a message on the beautiful card. Cecilia hoped deep in her heart that it was for her.

On February fourteenth, Miss Malone announced to the class: "Today when we have finished our lessons, we'll choose the best decorated box. Then you may deliver your valentines."

Cecilia could hardly concentrate on her work. She read the same paragraph over and over. The other students were fidgety and talkative. Realizing the futility of keeping the students' attention, Miss Malone finally told them to clear their desks and take out their decorated boxes. She walked down each aisle holding up box after box for all to see. Each student wrote the name of his favorite box on a small piece of paper.

"Clory, will you collect the votes for me?" Miss Malone asked. When all the votes had been collected and tallied, Miss Malone announced the winner: "Beatriz Apodaca!" Beatriz screamed with delight and ran up to receive the shiny pen.

"I didn't want that old pen anyway," said Belle. "My father will buy me a better one." But no one paid attention to her.

Miss Malone had another surprise for her students. She gave each one a red heart-shaped lollipop. This was a real treat for the farm children. Most couldn't afford store-bought candy.

Cecilia hugged her valentine box to her chest as she walked home with Belia. The two sisters went straight to their room to read their cards. Cecilia searched through her box, digging deeper and deeper, but found no special card from Johnny. Just the same little card he had made for Belia and all the others.

Who is going to get that card? Cecilia wondered. Could it be Belle, the class flirt? Estela, the class beauty? Or Jesusita or

Herlinda or Virginia? Would she ever know? With all these questions swirling in her head, Cecilia put away her valentines and went to the kitchen to help Tía Sara roll out tortillas for supper.

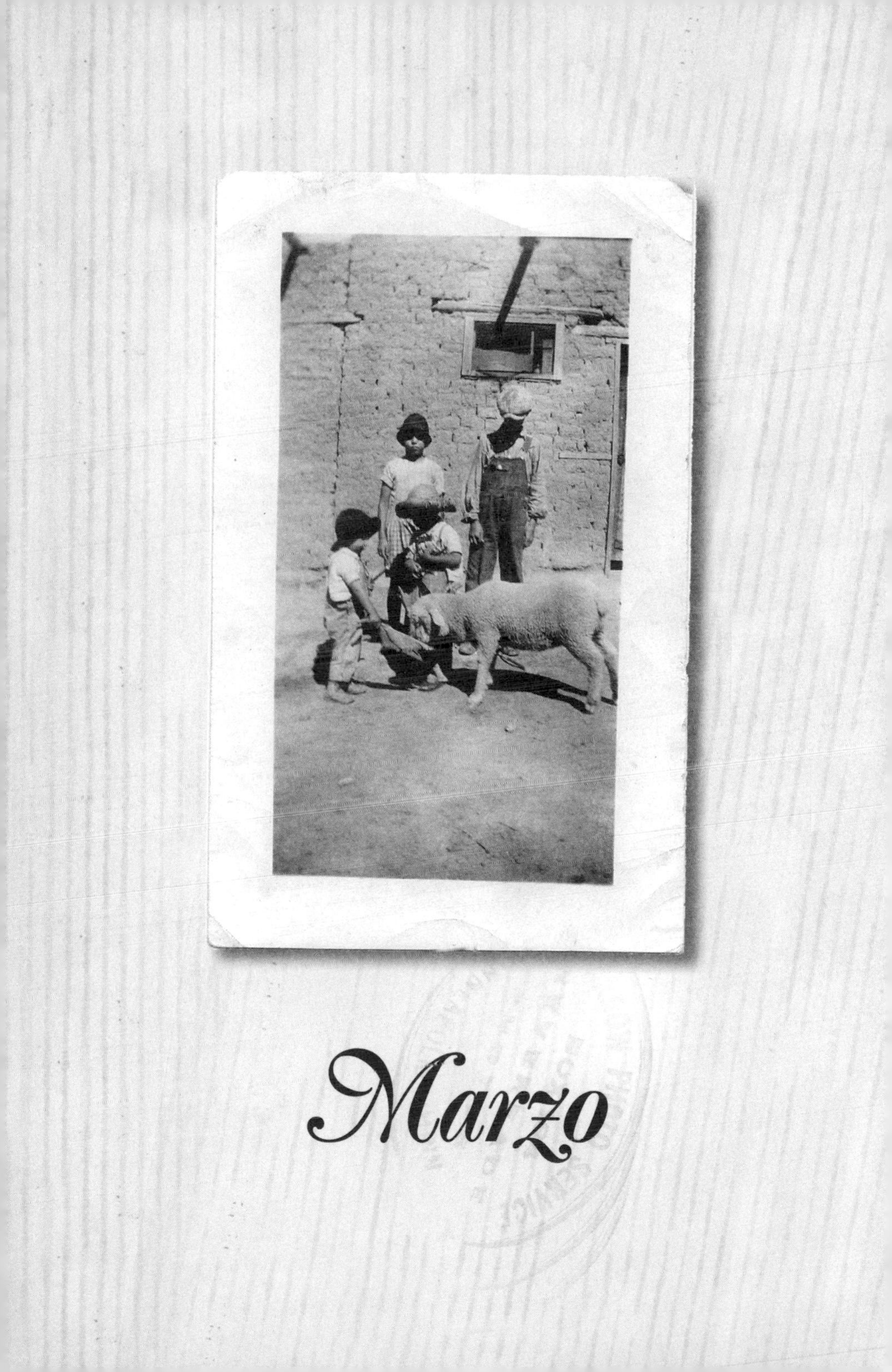

Marzo

March did not roar in like a lion. This year, the first day of March was balmy and sunny. Fito and Roberto rejoiced as they ran home from school barefoot. They tied their leather boots together by the laces and slung them over their shoulders. Tomorrow the cold might return, but today they could enjoy the feel of the warm earth on their bare feet.

Cecilia took her time walking home. The warm sun felt good on her back. She had been cold for so long. Surely, spring was near. In fact, this morning she heard baby birds chirping in a nest in the eaves outside her window. And today, a bee flew into the schoolroom, throwing all the girls into a panic.

The spelling bee! Remembering the pesky bee turned her thoughts to the forthcoming competition. March was the month of the school spelling bee. The winner would get to compete against all the winners from the neighboring towns at the high school in Hot Springs. Cecilia wanted to win. This was her last chance, since she would be graduating from eighth grade this year. The winner would receive a new high school dictionary. Imagine! A dictionary of her own! Cecilia dreamed of the heavy book filled with so many wonderful words. She could imagine her hands stroking the smooth pages and her eyes skimming across the fine print. Maybe the cover would have shiny gold letters. It didn't matter, as long as it was hers.

Some of the students in the class were staying after school to drill over the official list of words with Miss Malone. But Mamá would not give Cecilia permission to stay after school. She needed Cecilia at home to help with the housework. So Cecilia had been staying up late studying new words on her own. She had gotten so little sleep lately that now the warm sun made her feel drowsy. Her eyes were heavy-lidded. She longed for sleep. Maybe she could take a little nap before she started her chores. She slipped into her bedroom and lay on her bed, just to rest her eyes for a moment.

"Cecilia! Cecilia! Get up! It's time to get ready for school!" Cecilia heard Belia's urgent voice as from a far off distance.

"*¿Qué pasó?* What happened? Is supper ready?" Cecilia asked groggily, sitting up in bed. She realized with a start that she was still fully dressed and a blanket had been thrown over her. Oh, no! It was morning! Not only had she not helped with supper, she hadn't eaten any either! She had slept all afternoon and all night. Mamá must be furious! She jumped out of bed, ran to the dresser and poured water from the pitcher into a bowl. She splashed cold water on her face, dried it with a piece of flour sacking and hurried to the kitchen.

Mamá was standing at the stove. Without turning around she said, "Tía Sara had to do your chores yesterday. You owe her an apology. From now on, you will go to sleep with the rest of the family. I forbid you to stay up later. You are only wasting coal oil, and then you are good for nothing the next day." She placed a pan of oatmeal on the table with a bang.

Cecilia felt tears stinging her eyes. She said nothing, but began to set the table and pour the milk. Mamá was not being fair. Why hadn't someone woken her up? And if she didn't stay up late night after night, how would she ever get her homework done, or study for the high school entrance exam, or read her beloved books?

Tía Sara brushed aside the curtain in the doorway and came into the kitchen. Cecilia threw her arms around her and buried her face in her aunt's chest.

"*Lo siento*, Tía. I'm sorry. I didn't mean to fall asleep," she said, barely controlling her tears.

"*Está bien, niña. Está bien. Las intenciones son las que valen*. I know your intentions are always good. Now go get the baby ready for her breakfast," Tía Sara said with her usual gentleness. Cecilia hurried to do as she was told and to escape from Mamá's accusing silence.

At breakfast Mamá announced, "Lent is beginning. We need to order new clothes for Easter from the catalog. All of you come home straight from school. I need to take measurements."

"*¿Para qué necesitan ropa nueva?*" asked Papá. "Why do they need new clothes? School will be over in a few months."

"*Se pone uno lo mejor que tiene cuando visita la casa del Señor,*" said Tía Sara. "You have to wear your best when you visit the house of the Lord."

"Well, don't spend too much. I need to pay the bank loan this month," Papá warned as he swallowed a gulp of hot, fragrant coffee. The cup hid the worried look on his face.

"I've been doing some sewing for the neighbors. I have a little money saved up," replied Tía Sara. "I'll help pay for the clothes."

"*Hermana,* you don't have to do that. You do enough for us as it is," said Mamá. Papá grunted in agreement.

"It is my privilege. You are my family," Tía Sara insisted as she put her hand over her sister's. *"Son mi familia."*

Mamá and Tía Sara had only coffee for breakfast. During Lent they fasted for breakfast and dinner and ate only a light lunch. No one in the family would eat any type of meat during the entire Lenten season.

"I told Santiago we would go to his farm Saturday for the children to see the baby goats," said Papá. The children screamed with delight. Tío Santiago, Mamá's brother, had a goat farm and playing with the baby goats was a spring treat.

On Saturday the family walked the few miles on a dirt road to Tío Santiago's farm. Mamá and Tía Sara carried parasols to shield their faces from the March sun. The boys ran ahead throwing stones and chasing each other. Cecilia and Belia could not run with the boys. They had to walk sedately next to Mamá wearing their sunbonnets. When they got to the farmhouse, they were greeted by several frisky, barking dogs. Hearing the commotion, Tía Margarita, Santiago's wife, came out to welcome them. She was small and round with eyes that squinted when she smiled.

"*¡Bienvenidos! Pasen, pasen.* Come in. Santiago just brought in a pail of fresh goat milk. I'll pour everyone a glass," Tía Margarita said. Mamá cast a stern look at her children. Most of them hated goat's milk, but they would have to drink it out of politeness. Cecilia held the warm, foamy, strong-smelling stuff to her mouth and took several sips. She and Elías exchanged pained glances. What else could they do? They had to drink it. Fito and Roberto swallowed theirs in one big gulp and ran outside to play with their cousins, Leo and Raymundo. Belia actually liked goat's milk and drank two glassfuls. Then she and her cousin Elena went off to exchange secrets. There were no cousins Cecilia's and Elías' age, so they sat with the adults in the small parlor until everyone went out to the pasture to see the goats.

The baby goats were adorable. There were at least twenty of them jumping and rearing up on their hind legs. When they saw the children invade their pasture, they ran toward them, heads lowered. They repeatedly butted the children's legs with their soft stubby horns until the children fell on the soft grass in laughter. The boys ran in mock terror as the tiny animals chased them with lowered heads, ready to butt anyone they could catch.

As the family took their leave with hugs and kisses all

around, Tío Santiago told Papá, "*Cuñado, ten cuidado*. Be careful. I heard from Samuel Apodaca that gypsies were seen in Hot Springs. They might come down this way."

Papá laughed. "*Bueno*, we'll lock up the children," he said jokingly. But Mamá looked worried. In her opinion, gypsies caused nothing but trouble. And Papá's joke about the children sent shivers down her spine. How could he laugh about it? Everyone knew gypsies would steal anything that wasn't locked up or nailed down—including children! She had heard many terrible stories of babies that had been left on a sunny porch for a few unguarded minutes while the mother went to check on the *cena*. The poor mother would come back to find the crib empty and her child gone forever! It seemed that everybody knew somebody who knew someone else who heard that this had happened to a cousin of a neighbor. Gypsies in the neighborhood meant pies could not be left on windowsills to cool, chickens would have to be penned up in the day as well as at night, and all farm tools had to be locked up in the barn. The family dogs would be left out at night to scare off any prowlers with their barking. One would just have to trust in *Dios*.

Several days later on a breezy Saturday afternoon, a strange dark woman appeared in the garden in front of the kitchen door. Cecilia watched her from behind the curtained window. The woman held a large bundle of brightly colored cloth.

"Mamá, there's a woman in the yard," Cecilia said.

Mamá looked out and muttered below her breath, "Gypsies." Cecilia was disappointed. This woman looked very ordinary, although it was obvious she was not from the neighborhood. Cecilia had seen pictures in books of gypsies wearing swirling skirts, bright colors, and large hoop earrings. But this woman was dressed very plainly in a worn brown dress and shabby brown shoes. She wasn't wearing any jewelry at all. The gypsy woman stood waiting to be acknowledged. Mamá stepped out onto the porch.

"*Buenas tardes,*" she said.

"*Buenas tardes,*" the gypsy answered.

"*¿Cómo puedo servirle?* How can I help you?" Mamá asked as she placed her hand on Cecilia's shoulder as if to keep her near. Cecilia noticed that Mamá spoke politely and formally to the woman.

"I have some sewing I need done. I heard a good seamstress lives here. I need some skirts made, lots of ruffles, lots of ribbons. I'll pay good money. I need them in a week," the woman explained.

"Go get your Tía Sara," Mamá ordered Cecilia. When Tía Sara appeared, the gypsy woman repeated her request and showed Tía Sara the large bundle of cloth. Tía Sara fingered the fine fabrics. There were silks and satins of beautiful strange colors Cecilia had never seen before. Deep purples, oranges, reds—the colors of Mamá's garden in spring. The gypsy explained how she wanted the skirts made. She needed a dozen. The women and girls of her camp would wear them at a gathering they were traveling to—a gypsy festival. Tía Sara agreed on a fee, and the woman slipped away as quietly as she had appeared, her brown coloring blending in with the road.

Together Tía Sara, Mamá, and Cecilia admired the beautiful lustrous fabrics the gypsy woman had left. These were the colors Cecilia had imagined gypsies wore.

"This fabric must have cost a fortune," Tía Sara said with awe. "*Será un placer trabajar con esta tela*. It will be a pleasure to work with such fine material."

"Can you make twelve skirts in one week?" Mamá asked. "And with all that trim? *Es mucho trabajo*."

"*Pasito a pasito se va muy lejos*. I'll have to finish them, one at a time. She's going to pay me very well," Tía Sara answered. "We can use the money to pay for Easter clothing for all of us."

During the next week, Tía Sara worked feverishly round the clock, running seams and gathering waistbands on the full skirts. Sewing the ruffle and ribbon trim was the most difficult because the satin material was slippery. Cecilia and

Belia helped by doing hand stitching wherever necessary. They also took over some of Tía Sara's duties around the house so she would have more time to sew.

During the week, Elías, Fito, Roberto, and the other boys of the town hung around the gypsy camp on Señor Tafoya's land. He had given the gypsies permission to camp there and use water from his pump. "Always better to stay on their good side," he said. Of course, the boys were at the camp without the knowledge of their mothers. Every one of them had been warned to stay away from the camp, but the lure of these strange and exotic people was too great.

The gypsies traveled in wagons and by horseback. They lived and slept in their covered wagons and in tents. Their camp was filled with smoke from their fires, barking dogs, and grubby children dressed in ragged clothing. The children may have been dressed in rags, but they looked plump and well fed with ruddy cheeks and bright dark eyes filled with curiosity. The camp was a busy place, bustling with noise and activity—men were shoeing horses, women were singing as they stirred pots over their campfires, and children were running and shouting. The gypsy boys showed Fito and Roberto their hunting knives, slingshots, and fishing poles. Roberto traded some marbles for a hand-carved slingshot. Mamá would have been furious if she had known. The gypsy women gave them flat round bread to eat, warm from the griddle on the campfire. What fascinated Elías the most were their horses—strong sleek creatures with shiny coats grazing on the grass around the wagons. He was amazed at the gypsy way of riding—no saddle, just bareback. Elías would go back home every evening and tell Cecilia about all the strange things he had seen. But he never mentioned the beautiful young gypsy girls who stared at him brazenly and smiled at him with painted lips.

"Why are you sewing for the gypsies?" Tía María asked Tía Sara angrily. "Don't you know the *gitanos* will just cheat you? What a fool you are! *No seas tonta.*"

Tía Sara went about her sewing. She had entered into a bargain in good faith. *Dios* would watch over her.

"*Haz bien y no mires a quién.* We should be good to everyone," Tía Sara told her sister-in-law.

One evening, a gypsy man came to the kitchen door. He rapped loudly, frightening the children.

"I need a *sobador*. I heard one lives here," he said politely. Papá was a *sobador*. Everyone came from miles around to have Papá massage their hands, arms, feet, backs, necks, or whatever part was sore and out of joint. Papá came out on the porch and invited the man to sit on one of the benches.

"*¿Dónde le duele?*" he asked the man. "Where are you in pain?"

"My wrist," the gypsy answered. "My hand got caught in my horse's bridle and my wrist was wrenched."

Papá got his bottle of massage oil, *Aceite de Volcânico*. This was a pungent smelling lotion he used to rub into achy joints. Sometimes Mamá would rub it on the children's chests when they had a cold and then cover their chests with a piece of flannel. Ugh! They could hardly sleep for the smell. Papá poured some oil on his palms and began to massage the gypsy's hand and wrist. The gypsy puffed on a cigarette.

"How is the farming here?" he asked Papá.

"We get by. This year was dry," Papá answered.

They talked on of other matters that interest men. Finally, the gypsy, already feeling better, rose and asked, "*¿Cuânto?* How much?"

"*Nada, nada*. Nothing. *Estâ bien,*" said Papá.

Mamá, listening from the kitchen, was furious. That night in bed she chided him.

"Why didn't you charge him? You could have asked even a little bit, and it would have helped. Why do you give everything away? Even haircuts!" Mamá said angrily. Papá was the local barber. Every Saturday afternoon he cut men's and children's hair. Anyone who needed a haircut and didn't want to go all the way to Hatch, or who just wanted to join in on the conversation, came and sat on the long porch of the house. Papá charged nothing, and it made Mamá angry. But there was no changing him.

On the seventh day, the gypsy woman reappeared in the garden. As before, she simply stood there until her presence was noticed. Tía Sara and Cecilia carried out the neatly folded skirts. They were beautiful! Cecilia thought the woman would at least take one and shake it out to inspect it. Instead, she handed Tía Sara a little bag, took the skirts in her thin brown arms, and walked down the dusty road. Tía Sara and Cecilia went inside where Mamá was waiting expectantly.

"Did she pay you? Is it the correct amount? Did she cheat you?" Mamá asked impatiently.

Tía Sara opened the small leather pouch and poured out three gold coins. Gold! Real gold coins from Mexico. None of them had ever seen gold coins before. Cecilia looked with fascination at the bright circles in Tía Sara's palm. The gypsy hadn't cheated Tía Sara. She had paid her fairly and with real gold coins that could be spent or turned into jewelry.

"We will all have new Easter clothes this year—even the baby!" said Tía Sara excitedly. Cecilia thought she saw tears in Tía Sara's eyes.

The next day, the boys were disappointed to find the gypsy camp deserted and the gypsies gone. And every farmer and his wife found something missing. A hoe, a hammer, a bucket, a chicken—and Tío Santiago even lost a baby goat. Besides the Tafoya's, only one other farm seemed to have escaped the pilfering of the gypsies.

"You see, Josefina," Papá told Mamá. "We are repaid for our kindness. The gypsies were grateful and left us alone."

"*Gracias a Dios.* Let us give thanks to the Lord," said Tía Sara. "*El hacer bien nunca pierde.* One never loses by doing good."

At the end of the month the school spelling bee was held. Cecilia came in third. But she didn't mind at all because the winner who would go on to the county competition in Hillsboro was none other than Johnny Tafoya.

Abril

On the first day of April, a few days before Easter, two men drove into the farmyard in a shiny black car. Getting out of the car, they stood looking at the house, the barn, the animal corrals, and the storage shed. Dressed in black suits and white shirts, they were completely out of place in the farming community where all the men and boys wore overalls, bandannas, and straw hats.

Mamá looked out the kitchen window. "¿Cecilia, *quiénes son?* Who are they?" she asked her daughter. "*¿Serán del banco?*" She seemed worried. Men like this never visited the farm. Who could they be?

Cecilia joined her mother at the window and peered out. "That is Mr. Johnson from the bank in Hatch. I saw him when I went to town with Papá. I don't know the other man." Cecilia had accompanied Papá to the bank in Hatch many times to serve as a translator. Papá understood English, but going to the bank with all the educated, well-dressed people made him nervous. He needed Cecilia's help when he stumbled over an English word. Mamá never went to the bank. She left all that business to her husband.

Cecilia and Mamá continued to peek out at the men with anxiety. Mr. Coke Johnson had never come to the farm before. Cecilia knew he was the manager of the Hatch National Bank, and it was he who approved Papá's loan every year to buy seed and equipment. She wondered, *Why had he come?*

Echoing her thoughts, Mamá asked, "*¿Qué querrán?* What do they want?" Cecilia could hear the tenseness in Mamá's voice. She looked up at Mamá for reassurance, but saw only worry in her eyes. Mamá's face was paler than Cecilia had ever seen it.

"*No sé*. I don't know. Should I get Papá?" Cecilia asked.

"*Sí, sí*. But before you go, invite them into the *sala*. I will bring them *café*."

Cecilia went outside and invited the two gentlemen to sit in the parlor. Mr. Johnson and the other man thanked her and, removing their hats, went inside through the door that opened onto the long porch. They sat at the big round table to wait for Papá. When Cecilia returned with her father, the men were already drinking Mamá's strong hot coffee. Getting to their feet, they greeted Papá and extended their hands. Papá's hands still had dirt from the fields on them, and he wiped them on his overalls before he shook hands. Mr. Johnson began to speak.

"José, I've come to talk to you about your loan payment. The bank hasn't received a payment from you in over three months. This is Mr. Morgan, the bank's attorney. He's here to notify you that the bank is starting proceedings to foreclose on your farm. I'm very sorry to have to bring you this news." Mr. Johnson looked pained as he spoke the shocking words.

Foreclose? What did that mean? Cecilia looked at Papá. Ashen-faced, he stood crumpling his straw hat between his nervous hands. She had never seen that defeated look on his face before. Suddenly she was more frightened than she had ever been in her life.

"*¿Papá, qué pasa?*" she asked him frantically.

"*Ay, hija, lo peor,*" Papá said as the two men stood patiently with glum faces. Papá explained that the chile crop hadn't been profitable the last year due to insect damage, and he had been unable to make the last three payments on the bank loan. But he knew this year's crop would be better, and he was planning on plowing the fallow field to grow more cotton. He knew he could repay the loan if they would give him a chance. Cecilia turned to the men and translated Papá's words.

"José, I know we've done business for twenty years, but the bank has a duty to its shareholders. We can't just let debts slide. It wouldn't be fair or good business," Mr. Johnson said gently. Just then Mamá came to the door of the *sala* with Sylvia in her arms. Elías, Fito, Belia, and Roberto all stood behind her, all wearing frightened looks on their faces. They knew something was terribly wrong. Only the baby laughed and rattled her wooden toy.

Cecilia looked at her beloved family. If the bank foreclosed on their home, where would they go? What would become of them? This old house had been in Mamá's family for over fifty years. Cecilia's grandfather, Domenico Luchini had homesteaded this land when he was discharged from the Union Army after the Civil War. He had served his country proudly at Fort Union, and now his family was in danger of being thrown off their land! Poor Papá was stunned into silence. His limited command of English failed him. Nervous and frightened, he couldn't say anything in either English or Spanish.

Cecilia felt anger rising in her chest. It wasn't fair! She had to do something to protect her family. The injustice of it all gave her courage. She stepped forward bravely to face the two men, and then she spoke calmly and clearly.

"Mr. Johnson, I am only fourteen. But I will be in high school next year. I study very hard, and I make good grades. When I graduate from high school, I'll get a job and pay you back every single penny. Just give me a chance. Please don't take our home."

Mr. Johnson and Mr. Morgan, looking like undertakers in their dark suits and black ties, listened to Cecilia with serious faces. They didn't treat her as if she were a child. She was grateful for that at least. The two men stepped aside and spoke to each other in low voices. Then Mr. Johnson spoke.

"Cecilia, tell your father we will consider this matter further. We'll be getting in touch again soon. *Muchas gracias por el café,*" he said to Mamá. Then the two men left.

"*¿Por Dios, José, qué hacemos?* What are we to do?" cried Mamá, holding Sylvia tightly in her arms.

"*No sé, no sé.* I don't know. I need time to think," answered Papá. "I have to finish plowing. Elías, *hijo*, come with me. We have work to do." And he walked out, leaving Mamá and the children pale and silent.

"Maybe we can send back our new Easter clothes," suggested Cecilia, breaking the silence.

"*Ay, mi hija*, that wouldn't even begin to pay the debt on the farm. No, we will have our new clothes and wear them proudly on Easter Sunday," said Mamá. "Even if we don't have new clothes for the next five years!"

All night Cecilia lay awake in bed worrying about the foreclosure. To make matters worse, the high school entrance exam was scheduled for next week. She had to pass! She had to go to high school and pay back the debt!

On Easter Sunday, the family rose early and donned their new clothes. The spring day was gloriously sunny and warm. As Cecilia put on her new pink dress, she felt a renewal of her spirit and a hope rising in her heart. Surely things would work out. Surely *Dios* would help them keep the farm.

Mamá's garden was already blooming in brilliant colors. The petunias were vivid purple and pink. Yellow daffodils grew straight and proud. Papá and Elías had already planted onions, garlic, peas, carrots, and fava beans. The sweet smell of growing things filled the air. The cold windy winter was gone. This was the season of rebirth and renewal, and Cecilia felt a part of it.

Cecilia put on her new straw hat with the pink ribbon and joined the family in the wagon. Belia was sweet in yellow, clutching a little straw purse. The boys looked fine in their new cotton shirts and trousers. As they rode to the *Iglesia de San Isidro*, they all thought hungrily of the feast that awaited them at home. All of them were fasting as Mamá insisted they go to communion on Easter Sunday. Mass would be at least two hours long, and their stomachs were already grumbling.

Inside, the church was warm from the morning sun, and people crowded the pews. Men stood holding their hats along the walls and in the back of the church. It seemed as if the building could not hold one more person. Padre Arteta began the mass. People rose, sat and knelt. Candles sent their smoky fumes into the air. The altar boys swung incense burners, releasing a sweet heavy odor. Cecilia sat praying fervently to *San Isidro* to help her family in their trouble. She saw Mamá and Tía Sara fumbling with their rosaries, and Papá, hat in hands, sitting tense and still. The worried look on his face told Cecilia his mind wasn't on the priest's sermon.

Cecilia began to feel warm and dizzy. The smoky smell of the candles and the incense nauseated her empty stomach. She couldn't seem to get enough air. She felt she was suffocating. Desperate for fresh air, she stood up in the pew. Suddenly, the lights of the church seemed to go out, and a hot flushed feeling ran up her neck to her head. The next thing Cecilia knew, she was lying outside on the grass with Papá holding her head in his lap and Mamá fanning her with a prayer book. Her eyelids fluttered, and she tried to sit up.

"Just rest, *hijita. Descansa.* Don't try to get up yet," Papá said.

"*¿Qué pasó?*" Cecilia murmured groggily.

"*Te desmayaste.* You fainted, and Papá carried you out," Mamá said, still fanning Cecilia's face.

Cecilia closed her eyes again. She was overcome with humiliation. Everyone must have seen her faint and be carried out like a baby. Even Johnny! She would be the laughingstock of the school. Cecilia felt she could never face anyone again. She held back her tears for the sake of Papá and Mamá. They would worry about her if she cried, and they had enough to worry about right now. She would just have to be strong and overcome this as she did all her problems.

Once home, Cecilia was revived by the excellent Easter feast that Mamá and Tía Sara laid before the family. After saying grace, everyone ate hungrily of baked guinea hens, mashed potatoes, and of course, frijoles and chile. For dessert they ate *capirotada*, the traditional Easter dish made with bread, raisins, pecans, butter, and *piloncillo*, a brown sugar. Cecilia was so embarrassed from her faint that she ate only one heaping plateful of *capirotada* instead of two like the boys.

That night Mamá gathered the children together, and they all knelt in front of the statue of *San Judas*, the patron saint of hopeless causes.

"*San Judas*, please help us find a way to keep our farm," they prayed.

"And please help me and Elías pass the high school exam," Cecilia added under her breath.

On Monday afternoon, Fito came running across the field clutching the mail he had picked up at Tío Ben's store. "Mamá! Mamá!" he shouted. "There is a letter from the bank!"

Mamá and Tía Sara left the stove and rushed to the porch.

"Run and get your Papá. *¡Apúrate!*" Mamá ordered as she took the letter. Soon Papá and all the family members were gathered anxiously on the porch as Cecilia opened the letter and began to read the English words.

"Papá! Mamá! We are saved! The bank is extending the loan. It is not going to foreclose! We have another chance!" Cecilia shouted.

"*¡Bendito sea Dios!* Praise be to God!" Tía Sara exclaimed. Papá and Mamá embraced. Tía Sara grabbed Roberto and swung him around. Fito and Belia ran in circles around the others, whooping with joy. Elías stood silently, but his eyes were moist as he tried to hold back tears. Cecilia just stood clutching the letter, feeling her heart beat like a drum in her chest.

"*Gracias, San Judas*. Thank you," she whispered.

Three weeks later another letter arrived. The superintendent of county schools was pleased to inform Mr. and Mrs. Gonzales that their daughter María Cecilia had passed the high school entrance exam with the highest score in the county. However, their son Elías had failed by five points and could not attend high school until he passed the exam. Cecilia was ecstatic! The farm was saved and now this! All her prayers had been answered. Not only was she going to high school, but she had made the highest score. How proud Papá and Mamá must be of her! She looked at their faces with joy and expectation.

"*Ay*, Mamá, I will study so hard in high school next year. Then I can get a job and repay the bank loan," she said, finally admitting her plans to her parents.

"*No, señorita,*" said Mamá sternly. "You are not going to high school without Elías. He is a man, and his sister cannot go before him. He cannot lose face in the town. You will have to wait until Elías goes, and if he never goes, you cannot go."

Cecilia knew her mother meant every word. And she knew Papá always let Mamá make the decisions concerning the girls. How could she favor Elías in that way? Why did he always come first? Just because he was a boy! It wasn't fair! Things had always been this way, and it had never been fair.

Belle, Virginia, and Johnny would all be going to hig. school without her. Disappointment and despair engulfed her. Cecilia ran to her room and threw herself across the bed. She sobbed into her pillow. Her dreams were shattered and lay in pieces all about her.

Mayo

Cecilia seemed to sleepwalk to school the next morning. She had cried herself to sleep, and now her eyes were red and puffy. But she didn't care. She didn't care about anything. She hadn't even combed her hair properly, and loose wisps blew in her eyes as she walked. She had been through so much this year that now she felt numb and emotionally exhausted. She had studied so hard and worried so much about Fito, the farm loan, and the exam that now she didn't have the strength to worry about the future. Slipping quietly into her seat, she was oblivious to the noisy boisterous students around her.

"Children, settle down, please. Come to order!" Miss Malone said.

Cecilia, turning, caught Johnny's eye, and he smiled. She didn't smile back. Somehow, she couldn't make the effort.

"I have wonderful news for you," Miss Malone told the class. "Cecilia has passed the high school entrance exam with the highest score in the county. Congratulations, Cecilia!"

The students applauded, and some of the boys whistled shrilly between their teeth. At this moment, Cecilia should have felt happy and proud, but all she felt was despair. At lunch her friends hugged her and congratulated her. Even Belle grabbed her hand and said for all to hear, "What did you expect? Brains run in our family!"

Cecilia ate her bread and cheese outside under a tree. The bread stuck in her dry throat, and she could barely swallow. She walked to the pump for a drink of water and didn't even notice that Johnny had followed her.

"*Felicitaciones.* Congratulations, Cecilia," he said. She started in surprise.

"*Gracias,*" she answered.

"We'll have fun in high school next year, won't we?" Johnny asked, taking over the pumping. He filled a dipper of water and held it out to Cecilia.

"*Claro.* Of course we will," she answered without looking at him. She didn't have the heart or the energy to explain to him that she would not be going with everyone else.

"Maybe we can get together this summer and do some

extra studying—you know, get ahead a little bit. I could come to your house, if that would be all right with your mother," Johnny suggested. His excitement and anticipation were obvious.

"Yes, well, I'll have to let you know. I might be too busy. I don't know," Cecilia said awkwardly, stumbling over her words. She cringed with embarrassment and turned her face away so Johnny would not see the tears that had begun to form in her eyes.

"*Bueno,* I'll see you later," he said coolly and walked away.

Cecilia wanted to throw herself on the ground and cry her heart out, but all she could do with the whole school watching was walk sullenly back to her desk. She had hurt Johnny's feelings. She knew by that wounded and confused look on his face. He thought she didn't like him, that maybe she was just a flirt like Belle. What must he think of her? But how could she tell him the truth? She was overcome with humiliation. And there was Elías outside playing football and not seeming to care that he had failed the exam. If only she could be like him—satisfied with the way things were, with no passion in her soul for better things.

At three o'clock when Miss Malone dismissed the students to go home, she said, "Cecilia, may I see you a moment after school?" Cecilia stayed behind as the others filed out the door and broke into whoops of joy as they ran for home.

"Cecilia, I've been watching you. You don't seem as happy as I would expect you to be after scoring so highly on the exam. Is something wrong?" Miss Malone asked gently.

Cecilia could stand it no longer. She burst into tears as she tried to explain to Miss Malone about Elías and Mamá and the unfairness of life.

"Mamá says I can't go unless Elías goes, and Papá agreed. Mamá says I am wasting my time, and Papá says I should stay home and help Mamá in the house until I get married. Miss Malone, I don't want to stay home. I want to go to high school!" she said, choking back sobs.

Miss Malone put her arms around Cecilia and said, "Don't give up hope, sweetheart. We'll work something out. Surely there's a way."

"No, Miss Malone. You don't know my mamá. When she says something, she means it. Nothing will change her mind." Cecilia blew her nose into her handkerchief.

"I have an idea, but let me make a telephone call first. Ask your parents if I may visit them after school tomorrow," Miss Malone told her.

Cecilia walked home with dragging feet thinking about Miss Malone's words. Could it be possible that there was a solution? But what? How? Cecilia was old enough to know that life wasn't a fairy tale, and there wasn't always a happy ending. What she needed now was a miracle. Cecilia entered the house quietly and tried to slip into her room without being seen. She was too sad and depressed to talk to anyone. But Mamá was sitting on Cecilia's bed waiting for her.

"*Ven, mi hija. Mira lo que te tengo.* I have something for you," Mamá said. "Come see."

Mamá held out something black and velvety in her arms. It was a black shoulder cape decorated with black satin piping and bright silver beads sewn in a floral pattern across the front. Cecilia had never seen anything as lovely.

"*¡Qué hermosa!* How beautiful!" Cecilia exclaimed. She took the cape and ran her fingers over its velvet smoothness. "It's the most beautiful thing I've ever seen!"

"This is a special cape," Mamá explained. "Your *abuelo* bought it for me when I was eighteen years old. He bought one for your Tía Sara, too. We wore them when your *abuelo* took us all the way to El Paso to see President Taft meet Porfirio Díaz, the President of Mexico in 1909. We were so excited! Sara and I had never been farther than Las Cruces, and now we were going to El Paso to see the President of the United States and the President of Mexico meet for the first time in history. *¡Qué emoción!*"

"We caught the train in Rincón, and when we arrived in El Paso, we were shocked by all the people. We had never seen so many people in our lives! Hundreds of people were in the streets carrying banners and waving flags from both countries. Bands were playing, groups of schoolchildren were singing—the noise was incredible. There was a twenty-one-gun salute. Sara and I had to put our hands over our ears! And the decorations! They were so beautiful! Every building had ribbons and flags representing both countries. Even the horses wore feathers and ribbons. We stood in *Plaza de San Jacinto* and waited for the Presidents to arrive.

"When the procession rode by," Mamá continued, "we waved and shouted with everyone else. We actually got to see the two presidents! Porfirio Díaz was dressed so elegantly—*muy elegante*. He wore a military uniform decorated with medals, and he had gold lace at his throat. His hat had a big white plume. And President Taft—well, I've never seen any man as big. *¡Qué enorme!* Sara and I could hardly believe we were actually there. Imagine seeing such important men! Sara and I enjoyed the excitement so much—all the people, the bands, the decorations. And we got to wear our beautiful new capes. We felt so stylish and grand. This has always been one of the most exciting moments of my life—after my wedding day, of course.

"I saved my cape for my first-born daughter. That is you, Cecilia. I want you to have my cape as your own, to pass on to your own daughter someday," Mamá said.

Cecilia listened to Mamá's story with tears in her eyes. How she loved Mamá! She knew her mother was giving her the cape to let her know that she loved her despite not allowing her to go to high school. Cecilia threw her arms around Mamá's neck.

"*Gracias*, Mamá. I'll treasure it forever. All the girls will envy me, especially Belle!" Mamá and Cecilia laughed together at the thought of Belle. Then Cecilia had a sobering thought.

"Mamá, Miss Malone would like to talk to you and Papá after school tomorrow. May I tell her you will see her?" She waited for Mamá's answer. "*¿Está bien?*"

Mamá knew immediately the purpose of the visit. She hesitated before answering. She did not really want to see the teacher, but she had been raised a lady and knew her manners.

"*Claro que sí*. Tell Miss Malone she may visit tomorrow," Mamá finally said to Cecilia's overwhelming relief.

"Now go to the barn and help Belia feed the baby goats. She is waiting for you."

Cecilia ran with a lightened heart to the barn where Belia had already taken three baby bottles filled with goat milk. Lying in the hay were three white newborn goats, bleating with weak little voices.

"Aren't they adorable?" said Belia. Her greatest joy was taking care of baby animals on the farm. This spring she had a baby pig named Lola that followed her everywhere, even to school. Cecilia took a bottle and held it so one of the kids could suck from it. The goats were triplets, a very unusual occurrence. Their mother didn't have enough milk for three, so Cecilia and Belia fed them from bottles. In a few weeks, they would be eating hay on their own. Like the baby chicks Cecilia had cared for last summer, the kids would grow and become adult goats. Time seemed to pass so quickly; this year had flown by. Cecilia soon would be an adult woman herself. She wondered, *What will my life be like?* But the future looked dim and cloudy, and Cecilia turned her attention once again to the hungry goats.

Miss Malone walked briskly by Cecilia's side. She hadn't said a word about the visit all day. Cecilia wondered nervously what Miss Malone planned to say to her parents. She took her teacher into the *sala* where Mamá greeted her politely and invited her to sit down. She poured coffee into one of her best china cups and offered it to Miss Malone. It was an honor to have a teacher visit their home. Papá came in early from the fields. He had washed his face and hands and now sat awkwardly across from Miss Malone.

"I understand you feel Cecilia should not advance to high school without Elías. I quite understand. I have a proposition for you. I have received permission from the superintendent of schools to tutor Elías after school and on Saturdays. The superintendent will allow Elías to retake the test in two weeks. If he passes, will you allow Cecilia to attend high school next year?" the teacher asked.

Papá and Mamá exchanged looks. If Elías had to be tutored after school and even on Saturdays, he would have less time to help on the farm. Papá could not afford to hire a helper. But he also wanted to see his oldest son go to high school with the other boys. Papá thought for a long moment.

Cecilia sat with her heart in her throat. Her whole future depended on this moment. What if Papá and Mamá really didn't want her to go to school even if Elías passed the test? What if they really felt it was a waste of time for a girl to be educated? Cecilia held her breath.

Finally, Papá spoke in broken English. "You are very kind and generous to give my son your time. If Elías can pass the test, Cecilia may go to high school."

Cecilia let out a long sigh of relief. She wanted to scream and cry and jump for joy, but she knew she had to behave like a young lady. Instead, she rose from her chair and put her arms around Papá.

"I am so glad!" said Miss Malone, smiling broadly. "Cecilia is the smartest student in the class. She is going to be the valedictorian. You should be very proud of her." Miss

Malone rose and shook hands with Papá and Mamá.

"I will talk to Elías and set up a schedule for tutoring. We will begin right away."

Cecilia walked Miss Malone to the front gate. She felt as if she were walking on air. "Oh, Miss Malone, how can I ever thank you?" she asked, eyes glowing.

"Just study hard and learn all you can in high school. Strive to do your best always," Miss Malone said. "And don't forget to invite me to your high school graduation!"

At school, Johnny continued to behave distantly toward Cecilia. She knew she had hurt his feelings, but didn't know how to make amends. She was too embarrassed to explain her predicament. No one except the family knew Elías had failed the exam and that Miss Malone was tutoring him for a retake. If only Elías would pass the test! Again Cecilia lit candles at the church and said prayers to her favorite saints. They had helped her before. Perhaps they would help her again.

Day after day, Elías stayed after school for Miss Malone to review English grammar and mathematics with him. This time he genuinely wanted to pass the test. He was embarrassed to realize the other boys would go on to high school while he would be left behind. Besides, he wanted to be on the high school football team. At night after all their chores were done, Cecilia would help him with his homework. She patiently explained difficult math problems and reviewed the tenses of irregular verbs.

"I know you can learn these verbs, *hermano*. You just have to memorize them," Cecilia said late one night.

"*Sí, claro,*" said Elías. "I need to memorize them. But it's not as easy for me as it is for you. It's hard for me, and I don't really want to do it."

"Elías, please try," she begged.

"I will, *hermanita*. I will try my best," he replied as he playfully pulled on her braid.

"Promise?" she said.

"*Te lo prometo*. I promise," he answered.

Miss Malone had received permission to administer the makeup test herself in the schoolroom. She would have to send it to Hot Springs to be graded. Elías took the test on a Saturday morning when he would much rather have been riding Panky, his favorite pony. He tried to concentrate as hard as he could because he had promised Cecilia. He knew how important this was to her. He didn't want to let her, or Miss Malone, down. He scratched his head and chewed the end of his pencil. He squinted his eyes and frowned until he developed a headache. After working for two hours, he handed the test to Miss Malone. She sealed it in a large manila envelope and mailed it on Monday morning. The only thing left to do was wait.

Cecilia never knew how she made it through the next week. She felt giddy and scared at the same time. She and Miss Malone had done their best, and Elías had studied hard. If he didn't pass now, he never would pass. And there would go her dreams of making a better life for herself and her family.

Tía Sara came into Cecilia's room one night as Cecilia knelt by her bed praying the rosary. She knelt next to Cecilia and finished praying with her.

"*Ay, Tía*, I'm so tired of worrying," Cecilia told her. "Maybe I should just give up and forget about high school."

"*¡Nunca!*" Tía Sara admonished her. "*La esperanza es lo último que se acaba*. You must *never* give up hope!"

Cecilia thought of her favorite Greek myth about Pandora's box. Pandora had opened the box, releasing all the evils of the world. But at the bottom of the box lay one last winged creature—Hope.

A week later, the day before the end of school, Miss Malone came to the farmhouse after school carrying an envelope. The family gathered in the *sala*, and Miss Malone read the letter aloud.

"The superintendent is pleased to announce that your son Elías has passed the high school entrance exam with a grade of 75. He will be promoted next year!"

Elías stood proudly. Cecilia clasped her hands together. "*Gracias, San Judas. Gracias, Santa Cecilia. Gracias, Virgencita,*" she said. But Miss Malone knew it was also everyone's hard work that had paid off. She hugged Elías and then Cecilia.

"I expect you two to graduate from high school with flying colors!" she told them.

"Thank you so much for everything, Miss Malone," said Cecilia.

"*Sí, muchas gracias,*" said Papá. "*Lo agradecemos mucho.*"

Now Cecilia could go back to school with a light heart. Now she could discuss high school with her friends and make plans. But what about Johnny? Would he ever forgive her for her seeming indifference to him?

On Friday, the last day of school, the class held a small celebration. Miss Malone passed out candy as the students went to her desk to receive their report cards. On Saturday morning, a simple graduation ceremony would be held at school honoring Cecilia, the valedictorian, and Hector Ogaz, the salutatorian. Cecilia would wear her pink Easter outfit. She walked home mentally rehearsing the speech she would give at graduation.

"Cecilia, wait! *¡Espérame!*" She turned to see Johnny running toward her. She had avoided him all week, and now she stood waiting and wondering what he wanted.

"Cecilia, I want to congratulate you for being valedictorian. *Felicitaciones.* I hope we'll still be good friends next year in high school, now that you are going after all," said Johnny with a sly smile.

"How did you know?" Cecilia asked, eyes wide with confusion.

"Belle told me. I asked her why you were acting so strangely, and she said it was because of Elías and the test and everything," Johnny explained. Cecilia felt herself blush. She should have known Belle could never keep a secret.

"Oh, Johnny, I'm sorry if I was rude to you. I didn't know what to say about studying together, but now if you still want to, I would love to study with you this summer," she said. She blushed even redder for she had never said anything so forward in her life.

"*Seguro que sí,*" Johnny said. "By the way, I have something for you. I made it a long time ago, but I was too scared to give it to you."

Johnny pulled the beautiful valentine he had made from his book bag. Cecilia took the valentine in her trembling hands.

"It's so beautiful! Thank you, Johnny. I'll keep it forever!" she said. And then Johnny did something quite unexpected. He leaned forward and kissed Cecilia very quickly on the cheek. Then he let out a big whoop and ran down the road toward his house.

Cecilia watched Johnny until he was just a dot in the distance. She clutched the big red valentine to her heart. She stood looking at the purple and blue mountains of her valley, and she thought of all the things that had happened to her this year—all the fears and the worries and all the hopes and dreams she had nurtured. All her dreams had come true after all, and next year she would be starting a new life. And after that, well, who knew what could happen? She would just have to wait and see. But one thing she knew for sure, she would never stop dreaming and hoping. She thought of Tía Sara's wise words: *Con paciencia se gana el cielo.* With patience and hope, anything is possible!

Authors' Note

Cecilia Gonzales is a real person who really did grow up on a farm in Derry, New Mexico. Cecilia's dream was to get an education and to make a better life for herself and her family. Through determination and hard work, she was able to see this dream come true.

Cecilia graduated as salutatorian from Hatch Union High School in Hatch, New Mexico, in 1938. Against her mother's strong protestations, she left the family farm for El Paso, Texas, where she attended the International Business College. She paid her tuition and supported herself through secretarial work, including working for the well-known architects, Trost and Trost. During World War II, Cecilia worked for the Office of Alien Registration under the Department of Justice and for the Post Quartermaster at Fort Bliss, Texas. Because she was bilingual, she was hired by the U. S. Office of Censorship, where she monitored telephone calls between El Paso and Latin America during the war.

In 1944, Cecilia left El Paso for New York City to marry her husband, Anees Abraham, a native El Pasoan. He had joined the army and was stationed in Pennsylvania. They were married for forty-nine years. While in New York, she worked for the American Red Cross, where she met Mayor La Guardia and First Lady Eleanor Roosevelt.

In 1964, Cecilia became one of the first employees of the Chamizal Project under the U.S. Boundary and Water Commission. She served as a hostess during the transfer of the Chamizal to Mexico where she met President Lyndon B. Johnson of the United States and President Díaz Ordaz of Mexico. In 1967, she was the first employee of the Chamizal National Memorial in El Paso, Texas. She met First Ladies Rosalynn Carter of the U.S. and Sra. Carmen Romano López Portillo of Mexico during their visit in 1977.

Cecilia was assigned to take inventory of the LBJ Ranch home in Johnson City, Texas, before it was donated to the National Park Service by Mrs. Lyndon B. Johnson in 1968. Mrs. Johnson graciously met with Cecilia and the other Park Service employees, serving them coffee and cookies.

Besides meeting two Presidents and four First Ladies and retiring after over twenty years of government service, Cecilia has traveled all over the world to places such as South America, Europe, Greece, Turkey, Canada, the Caribbean, and Mexico—not bad for a young farm girl who used to sit daydreaming under a cottonwood tree.

Glossary of Dichos
(Proverbs)

El hombre propone y Dios dispone.
Man proposes, and God disposes.

Aunque la jaula sea de oro, no deja de ser prisión.
Even if a cage is made of gold, it is still a prison.

En boca cerrada no entra mosca.
A fly doesn't enter a closed mouth.

Todo lo que entra por los ojos es superficial. Lo que cuenta es lo que sientes con el corazón.
Everything the eyes see is superficial. What counts is what you feel in your heart.

Dios le da pan al que no tiene dientes.
God gives bread to those without teeth.

La flojera es madre de los atrazos.
Laziness is the source of setbacks.

Quien mucho duerme, poco aprende.
He who sleeps a lot learns little.

¿Qué culpa tiene San Pedro que San Pablo sea pelón?
What fault is it of Saint Peter that Saint Paul is bald?

Para todo hay remedio, menos la muerte.
There is a remedy for everything except death.

Hombre prevenido nunca será vencido.
A man who is prepared will never be defeated.

Al mal tiempo hay que ponerle buena cara.
During bad times you must wear a happy face.

De tal palo, tal astilla.
From such a stick comes such a splinter.

Los duelos con pan son menos.
It is easier to face your troubles on a full stomach.

Arco iris al amanecer, agua al anochecer.
A rainbow in the morning means rain in the evening.

Las intenciones son las que valen.
Intentions are what matter.

Pasito a pasito se va muy lejos.
Little by little one can go very far.

Haz bien y no mires a quién.
Do good without discriminating.

El hacer bien nunca pierde.
No one ever loses by doing the right thing.

La esperanza es lo último que se acaba.
Hope is the last to go.

Con paciencia se gana el cielo.
With patience heaven is won.